SAVER'S SAVIOR

BOOK TWO OF THE MAGICAL WAYS SERIES

BY: YASMINA KOHL

Yasmina Kehl

Yasmina Kohl

Published by ICB Publishing

Copyright 2011

Other books by Yasmine Kohl

Magical Ways Series:

Cassandra's Heart (Book 1)

DEDICATION

So the people I have to thank on this book of course include my husband who still is putting up with me and my crazy ass self.

My kids who are still hanging around, though the oldest will soon be joining the ranks of the United States Army. Please keep your feet on the ground and stay safe. But we are proud of you.

And for contributing to the delinquency of a writer: Lance and Shawn you two were my dirty little secret for months before I got the nerve up to tell you I had written in you into my book. Then you where so wonderful about it, it made my day.

Brodey, you are awesome and you rock...your name's in the book so now you have to buy it. MUWHAHAHAHAH honestly thank you for the help with what Xavier should imbibe.

Bill, your Shamrock Lover's is on its way, until then you'll just have to settle for the crew from Magical Ways a second time.

Betty, I worship your red pen...I fear it but I worship it to.

Kazyuyo, domo arigatō Kazu-son, and thank you Linda.

Stuart you are still awesome and you are still an ass, some day I will forgive you for pushing me into this, but not 'till I have a cabana boy.

AUTHOR'S NOTE

Please note this story was written before the world change:

The first change being the death of Osama bin Laden. Thank you for this change Seal Team 6. You are forever in our thoughts.

The second change is that this story was written before the repeal of Don't Ask Don't Tell, a stupid discriminatory law that should never have been in place.

I hope as I write the rest of the series there are other changes for the good in our world.

A bit about the Japanese in this book, Kazyuyo and her daughter Linda told me that in the Japanese culture they don't really do the endearment nickname thing, darling, honey, and sweetheart and such. But with Emiko trying to fit into her self-made American family, I think she would have picked up the habit. Besides I love the nickname koishii-chan. It's sweet and simple like Emiko.

CHAPTER ONE

"STOP! STOP! NO! NO DON'T! YOU DON'T UNDERSTAND! NO DON'T NOOOOOOOOO!"

Xavier bolted up right in bed. "Damn it! Fuck, didn't drink enough last night," he lay back down to keep the room from spinning. He might not have drunk enough to keep the nightmares at bay, but he had drunk enough for a hangover to slide in.

Ring. Ring.

"Damn it, go away."

Ring. Ring.

"Fuck."

Ring. Ring.

"What?!"

"Well, aren't you in a good mood. And I know you were taught better phone manners than that. I know this because I taught them to you."

"Mom."

"Yes, that is one of the many names I answer to. Though that tone used to get you grounded."

"Yes mother, my mother," Xavier said, parodying The Dead Poets Society scene.

"Don't start that shit with me, mister."

"Why are you darkening my ear drums?"

"Because it's too far to drive to do it to your doorway."

"What do you want? I was sleeping."

Sandra St.Clolud's heart sank. She kept hoping that one of these days her happy little boy would come back and this wounded man who snapped and hid in the dark would leave.

"Honey, it's 2:30 in the afternoon."

"I know what time it is. I can see and I can tell time."

"Xavier."

"Mother."

Sandra sighed and pushed on. "We need your flight info."

"Flight info?"

"Xavier."

"What?"

"Your flight home for Louise's wedding."

"I'm not coming."

Sandra sighed again, "Yes, you are."

"No. I'm not."

"Xavier, it's important to us that you come. We all miss you. We need to see you and know you're ok."

"Well I'm not, so why should I come and disappoint you all in person?"

"So you're not ok, but we still need to see you. We love you."

It was Xavier's turn to sigh. He knew they meant well; he just couldn't face them. They all wanted him to be okay, happy, like before and he couldn't, not after Lance and Shawn, and he knew he would never be okay again.

"Mom, I know you guys love me. I know you miss me. I just, I just, God I just can't. I…no matter what I do, I just feel raw and all the good memories there make everything even worse. It makes it hurt like it was yesterday, not three years ago. I need more time."

"Xavier, if you haven't come back after three years of more time, you're not going to. You need to go back to counseling; you need to go back to the PTSD specialist."

"It didn't help then and it won't help now."

"Baby, we only…"

"Want what's best for me, I know."

"Alright, be safe, we love you. Call if you change your mind about coming."

"Fine, bye."

His mom had stopped saying goodbye to him when he first started being deployed overseas. He had never told them where he was going or what he was doing but his mother knew, moms always know.

Xavier tried again to sleep the day away, but this time he was too awake, and everything he tried to keep out with sleep and alcohol flooded back.

"No, no, no, no, no, no." Xavier pounded his fist into his temples.

***

Xavier showered and shaved, his skin still red and raw from the blistering heat of the water, and out of habit, he grabbed his desert fatigues.

He felt out of place dressed in civilian clothes now…like a walking target.

He mindlessly put on his beat-up, worn-in, comfortable combat boots, grabbed the keys to his Jeep and made it as far as the doorknob before he froze with fear.

"Damn it, I'm a God damn combat trained Marine, trained to kill a man with my bare hands, and I've used that training," Xavier dropped his head to the door, "So why can't I walk out my own fucking door?"

Ring. Ring.

"FUCK!" With exasperation, he answered the phone "WHAT?"

"Master Sergeant St. Cloud?"

The fear in Xavier's body reached a critical state instantly. "What?" he said again, this time at barely a whisper.

"This is Lieutenant Markson. Colonel Snyder would like to see you in his office at oh-nine hundred tomorrow."

Called to the carpet three years after being discharged. This can't be good. "What is this regarding?"

"That will be discussed tomorrow at oh-nine hundred."

"I'm not coming in if I don't know what it's about. I've been discharged. I don't have to jump every time you guys call now."

"We understand that, Master Sergeant."

"Stop using my rank."

"Xavier, you will be in my office at oh-eight-four-five or I will be on your door step at oh-nine-fifteen."

"Yes, Colonel."

"Good, now stop giving Markson a hard time. He's a good man."

"They all are." Click.

It gave Xavier small satisfaction to be able to hang up on the Colonel. That was one benefit of being a civilian, and that simple pleasure of defying authority carried Xavier outside and to his car before it dawned on him that he was outside, sober, un-medicated and with no clue where he was going. "Son of a bitch, what the hell am I doing?"

"Son."

Xavier spun on his heel at the sound of a voice so close to him. He instantly changed his stance to fight but pulled short of attacking when it was a small elderly woman standing about eight feet from him. "Ma'am, sorry, didn't see you there. Pardon the language."

"No, son, it's fine, I've heard far worse. I was a Wave. Those boys could swear, oh boy could they, and some of them in more than one language. What branch?" She waved a hand towards his attire.

"Marine Corps."

"Didn't see too many Marines in my day."

"No ma'am."

"Good kids."

"Thank you, ma'am."

"So do you know what you're doing yet?"

"No ma'am. I have to buy a present for my sister's wedding. I don't shop much."

"What kind of gift are you looking for?"

"I have no idea," Xavier sighed, "I suppose something 'kitchen-y' - she likes to cook, well bake; she loves to make pastry stuff."

"Well son..."

"Xavier St. Cloud," Xavier interrupted the woman to introduce himself, a lifetime of ingrained manners overriding some of his anxiety.

"Margaret Thompson. Well, Xavier, there is a very nice shop on Main that sells all kinds of pastry stuff," Margaret chuckled. "Better ask for Nick. Nick will be able to help you sort through the large selection they have. It's called My Sweet Dream."

"Thank you Mrs. Thompson."

"Xavier?"

"Yes ma'am."

"Ms. And stop being so sad."

"Ma'am?"

"It's in your eyes; it's in the very air around you. You're alive. Remember that's a good thing."

"Yes ma'am."

"Good bye, Xavier."

"Good bye, Ms. Thompson."

Xavier watched the graceful woman walk to the stately BMW and drive away. "Well, it's something to go on."

CHAPTER TWO

"Emiko, Honey, time for your break," Yvette was angry when she saw Emiko jump like a frightened mouse at the sound of her soft voice.

"Hai," Emiko stopped. "Yes Yvette."

"See you in a bit," As Yvette watched Emiko walk away, she cursed the girl's parents yet again. She could never understand parents who would send their child away as a punishment and for something that was out of the girl's hands.

Yvette was the owner of Magical Ways, the clothing boutique where Emiko worked. Yvette knew Melissa was taking her to different places Asian men were likely to hang out. Melissa was playing matchmaker, hoping to find Emiko a better husband than the one her parents had picked for her. Melissa wanted to prove to Emiko's parents that Emiko didn't and wouldn't need their help ever again.

Yvette also had "the sight" as some called it. Yvette knew that Melissa wouldn't be the one to introduce Emiko to the person she needed in her life. Yvette

knew that it would be a terrible experience
for the girl but she hoped that any
resulting trauma wouldn't prove too much
for her small chéri. Yvette knew many
other things, like the fact that her girls
called her Mamma Yvette when she wasn't
there; they likened her to a mamma bear
protecting her young. She chuckled to
herself over that, because it was very true.
She also knew that the winds of change
were blowing around her small shop, and
as corny as that sounded even in her own
head, she knew it was all for the better
and as with all change, there would be
bumps and bruises, but then she knew
where the band-aids were.

"Yvette, you look great! How have
you been?" said a customer calling the
woman away from her thoughts.

***

"Yvette, Sandy is on the phone and
she wants you to come look at those
swatches."

"Oh shit. I completely forgot. Ok,
alright." Grabbing her keys and purse she
added, "Don't forget the deposit."

15 | P a g e

"We got it mom, go," Melissa quipped.

"You guys are hell on an ego, you know that, right?"

"Yep, of course we do," Anne answered.

Yvette laughed as she walked out the door, but when she rounded the corner where there were no windows to the shop, she stopped. *'Please lady, be careful with my littlest chéri. She can't handle much. And know if you break her I will hunt you down like the momma bear they all tease me about being.'*

Yvette felt you asked the gods for things, but in the end, you had better remind them where their place was…serving mortals. If you didn't, they got too big for their britches and started acting like politicians.

***

"Oh my gods, you would think it was the week before Christmas, not just some week in the middle of the damn month," Melissa whined, dropping into a chair.

"I know, this is crazy. Oh hell, it's almost five!" Anne exclaimed.

"Yeah."

"We haven't..." Anne started to remind Melissa.

"Oh shit, the deposit."

"And Yvette..." Anne again started to say something.

But was interrupted when Melissa added, "...said not to forget it."

"I will take the deposit," Emiko said stepping forward.

"Emiko, are you sure?" Anne asked the shy little Asian girl.

"Yes."

"Emiko?" Melissa wanted to be sure that she understood the girl.

"Yes, I am sure. I know the way, I want to help."

"Honey, you do," Anne tried to make the young woman understand.

"I know, but I can help more."

"I'll take it," Melissa piped up from the stock room getting her coat.

"No, you stay and clean, I will take it."

"Ok, if you're sure. Here's the bag and the bank's got the key, but it..." Anne handed the deposit bag over to the woman.

"Hai, I know the lock sticks."

"Yeah, it sticks."

"I am fine, you clean, go home. I will take the deposit to the bank. It is on my way home."

"Okay, if you're sure," Anne said once more.

"Yes."

Melissa and Anne watched the youngest and smallest of them all. "That was unusual."

"I know, she never volunteers for anything."

"She's so shy," Melissa stated.

"You're helping, she is getting better."

Melissa laid her head down on the counter, waves of fuchsia hair spilled out "I know, I know. But it's not enough, she won't talk to them."

"She wouldn't go in with you before," Anne pointed out while refolding a shirt on a display.

Melissa whined, "I know that too. I, gods, I just don't know what to do. We can't let her go home. They will treat her like a servant and she will never be happy. All her time will be spent playing the quiet, perfect obedient daughter. She is so strong, if she would only see it."

"Melissa, we can't force her, nor can we force the hand of the fates. We know she will be happy; she will be loved and cherished the way she deserves. She will be a mother and a wife."

"Anne, you should be a queen somewhere, you talk like one."

"Oh honey, I am in my own home."

"True, true, and you have your king charming."

"Oh, that is debatable at the moment. Do you know what he did last night?" Anne started to rant.

"Uh oh, what?"

"He actually ate the very last scoop of my double fudge chocolate chip mint ice cream."

"The bastard, the inhumane, unfeeling jerk. Get a rope - we'll string him up."

Anne laughing said, "Good thing we both have a sense of humor."

"Who's kidding?" Melissa said with a wicked gleam.

CHAPTER THREE

"What did she say was the name of that place...Sweetest Dreams...no, My Sweet Dream. Oh, okay there it is...damn, found it. Now I have to find a parking place. Shit, when the hell did I start talking to myself?" Xavier saw a parking spot about ten down from the shop he was looking for. He locked up his rag -top Jeep Wrangler and enabled the alarm. He stopped, took a deep breath, counted to ten, and tried really hard not to scream.

Since Afghanistan he had not been anywhere with more than ten people other than the hospital. Even then, there were never more than five people in his room at once.

He tried to remember all of the things the shrink had said to try to overcome his PTSD. None of it ever seemed to work though. His neck felt like it was on fire and crawling with a million ants, his chest felt as if there was an entire striker brigade sitting on it. Rubbing his neck and trying to breath past the pressure in his chest, he stepped up onto the sidewalk. He kept counting to ten in his head, hoping that something would just "click" and his life would be back.

"No, please no, please do not take the bag. Iie iie no, I need to keep it. Tasukete, tasukete help, help please!!"

"Lady if you don't shut the hell up and give me that bag I'm going to cut your damn throat."

Xavier stepped into the alley following the voices, "I wouldn't if I were you."

"What are you, her boyfriend or something?"

"Or something. We'll just say I'm a Special Forces trained vet they sent home for being too unstable to keep in combat."

The greasy little man raised and eyebrow and said, "Right, man."

Xavier saw the punch before the man moved but he let it make contact. He wanted to feel the pain. He wanted the adrenalin, wanted to use ir to get past the blocks he had been trying to build since waking up alive that day. He let the man hit him a few more times. A passing thought of *"When did I become a masochist?"* flew through his mind.

However, as soon as the thief laughed because Xavier was taking the punches, he snapped and hit the man twice.

When the guy finally woke up he would find himself about five feet from where he had tried to rob the woman, with Xavier's knuckle prints on his cheek and Xavier's palm print dead center on his chest. He would also find that he would have a headache from where his head bounced off the wall of the alley.

Xavier turned towards the woman and asked, "Miss, are you ok? Did he hurt you? Is there someone I can call, miss?" Xavier spoke softly. He had seen people's reactions to what he was capable of before. Few people could handle it well. Fewer still could accept it. "Miss, please, are you ok?" He brushed his hand up her shoulder.

"Emiko, oh God, oh God, Emiko, Emiko, oh, MELISSA! MELISSA! Emiko's hurt!"

Xavier turned toward the sidewalk in time to see a very small fist slam into his nose and to hear it crack. The next swing he caught. "Damn it woman, I didn't hurt her. He did," Xavier nodded toward the passed out would-be thief.

"Anne," Emiko spoke for the first time since calling for help.

"Emiko, oh thank heaven. Yvette would have my head if something happened to you," Anne said relived.

"Melissa, help me get her back to the shop."

"I'll do it," Xavier gently pushed the two women back, both of whom looked as if they were too small to pick up a bird, let alone a full-grown woman, even if she was a small Oriental woman. As he leaned over to pick up Emiko, he turned back toward the one he assumed was Melissa. "Your hair is pink."

"It's fuchsia, it's not pink, and so?"

"That's pink in a guy's book. Where to?"

"Follow me," Anne said walking back out of the alley.

Emiko was rigid in Xavier's arms. She had never been held in any way by a man. She didn't know what to do; she was more terrified now than she had been in the alley. There she was just trying to be less timid.

"I won't hurt you."

Confused Emiko said, "You hurt him."

"Because he was hurting you."

"Why would you protect me? You do not know me."

"Because I swore to protect everyone."

"It is your job?"

"Sort of," Xavier said with a small laugh.

The girl tilted her head up and Xavier saw her eyes for the first time. She had kept her head down, her chin buried in her chest. Her eyes were a soft chocolate brown with flecks of amber. He could feel her skin and it was as smooth as a baby's. "You are very pretty," he whispered. Immediately her head went back down hiding her eyes once more.

"Set her here. Thank you," Anne said pointing to a settee.

"Yes ma'am."

"Ma'am, wow, didn't think that word still existed in the English language," Anne declared.

"It does, ma'am. I don't know if she was hurt or just badly scared. You should call the police and let them pick up the mugger though. He might try again on someone else and succeed."

"Melissa is with him right now. She stayed to make sure if he woke up he didn't run off."

"Oh shit, she'll break like a twig," Xavier bolted up right and lunged toward the door.

"No, that twig is steel reinforced with a titanium shell."

"Excuse me?" The baffled man said.

"Melissa is a black belt in two separate forms of martial arts. She also has a wicked left hook, I hear."

Melissa walked in and said, "Plus I'm also a master with knots. The cops will be here in a few minutes, Emiko. They want to talk to you."

"I thought you were going to watch him?" Xavier asked becoming even more bewildered.

"I found some rope and tied him to the garbage can. When the cops come I'll untie him so they can take him."

Xavier finally took full stock of the girl. "You're all of what, twelve? How do you have two black belts and tie knots the cops won't be able to undo?"

Melissa laughed, Anne chuckled, and to Xavier's surprise, even Emiko giggled shyly.

"Where I was raised, knots were important to know and understand. And as an adult they became more important to me in my, let's say, personal life. I've tied knots that no sailor, Boy Scout or Eagle Scout could untie. Might be able to cut through them, but I pride myself on not giving any room for knives. More fun that way. As for the age thing...well looks can be and often are deceiving. And with that comes the time it takes to get two black belts."

CHAPTER FOUR

"Saver, what are you doing here?"

Xavier once again spun, ready to attack, but was able to kill the instinct faster than he had with Margret. "Sam, you're still hanging around here. Haven't moved on, huh?"

"No, not yet. Denise still has a year to go in school, then the wife and I are out of here. What happened, man?" Sam asked, not mentioning the look or the stance Xavier had taken at the sound of his voice, a voice he had known all of his life.

"I came to get something for Louise's wedding, and I heard a woman yelling for help and a guy telling her to give him the bag or he would cut her. I responded."

Sam had known the Marine for years; Xavier had gone to school with Sam's oldest daughter. Sam had a good idea what Xavier had been doing for the Corps along with Lance and Shawn before they had been killed.

The town they lived in had known without knowing, because of course no one could talk about special ops stuff. Sam saw the bruises forming on the vets face and figured there might be one or two under his shirt as well. "Saver, man, uh, hey look, I think I know what you're doing…I can also see the black eye you're going to have," Sam used the nickname Xavier had gotten years earlier hoping that it might help to keep the man calm.

Xavier shook his head. "Outside," He stood with his back to the wall and Sam toward the crowd. The adrenaline was gone, and he was now back to fighting his own mind. He counted to ten a half a dozen times, closed his eyes, trying to keep himself from freaking out. "Look Sam, yeah I let the guy hit me a few times. I don't know, I wanted him to hit me. I wanted the bruises. Fuck, I almost feel like I need them."

"Xavier, man you need to get back in therapy. If that army guy didn't help maybe you need to talk to someone else. Maybe, I don't know… a freelance guy. You know, maybe someone who isn't being paid by the military. 'Cause that sounds to me like you're still trying to get yourself killed."

"Oh come on, Sam, I knew he couldn't even hurt me. I just wanted the pain. Anything to get…" Xavier left the thought unsaid. Sam could understand. He had been in the first Iraq war; he had lost buddies.

"Xavier, you need to get past this man. You're not you. I can barely see you in there."

"I know," he said so quietly he almost didn't hear himself say it.

Sam ran a tired hand through his graying hair, "Look, the guy is a known druggy. He must owe his dealer a little more than usual 'cause generally he only snatches purses. Trying for a bank deposit is out of his league, even if you hadn't been there. Hey, when did you get so crazy with the knots, by the way?" Sam asked.

"I didn't, one of the woman's friends did. Something about growing up with them, think maybe she's into bondage or something."

"Oh, fun. We can't get the guy loose."

"Yeah, she said she would untie him when you got here."

"Okay, well let's get him out of here and have the girl checked out."

"I'm sure he didn't hurt her, just shook her up a lot. She seemed more scared. Not sure how much English she speaks either; when she was panicking she was speaking another language, I'd guess Japanese."

"Okay, well, Tom will have gotten all her info by now."

The two men returned to the store. Xavier saw Emiko in the same place he had left her. Anne was talking to a little old lady and Melissa was talking to Tom a few feet from Emiko.

He walked over to her and knelt down before her. Emiko lifted her head a little to see what he wanted.

"Are sure you are okay?" Xavier asked once more.

"Yes, thank you again for your help."

"No problem, miss. Be careful in the future," With that, Xavier rose and walked away.

***

Xavier woke up with a start as usual and, as was his routine, he cursed a blue streak. Half way to the shower, he stopped cold and cursed another one. Glancing at the clock, he figured he had five minutes to shower and fifty-five minutes to talk himself out the door. It would take him twenty minutes to get to the base. He still had his ID and base sticker, so getting on the base wouldn't be an issue.

He pulled up in front of the colonel's office with ten minutes to spare. He was impressed; maybe he just needed a reason to push himself out of the door. He briefly thought about getting a job but nixed it as his heart beat shot up into the stratosphere the second he stepped out of his Jeep and into a crowd of people. *'Coward,'* he thought to himself, *'there are only twelve people here.'* He made it to Snyder's office out of sheer will power, and with the last of it, he kept himself from slamming the door closed or turning the lock. He did, however, count himself lucky it was empty. He leaned against the wall and scrubbed his face with his hands.

Snyder could see St. Cloud through the barely open door, but said nothing. He quietly got up and poured two cups of coffee but added a good shot of whiskey to one. Regs be damned, St. Cloud would need it, especially for what needed to be said and done. When he figured he had given the boy enough time to deal with his inner demons he called out, "Markson, call Master Sergeant St. Cloud, he's about to be late," The colonel knew that Markson wasn't in the office; he had sent the boy on a supply hunt. Somehow this office was always short something, this week it was paper.

Xavier snapped to attention at the sound of the command, even though it wasn't for him. He started toward the phone, but he did manage to draw up short of calling himself. Scrubbing his face one more time, he stepped toward the door, opened it, and said, "He's not here, and I'm not late."

"I see that," the colonel turned from the credenza with the coffee and shoved one into St. Cloud's hand. "Drink," he barked.

Xavier reacted and then coughed, "Damn, when did they start adding whiskey to Marine coffee?"

"Since boys started coming home and hiding in the dark. We have to talk about this first."

Xavier barely caught the folder without dropping the coffee. He had an inkling of what would be in it. He had heard once the colonel's nephew was a detective on the force; he could have seen Xavier's name and slipped his uncle a copy of the file.

"It's a file," Xavier said trying to sound more cavalier than he felt.

"Open it."

"I know what's in it - paper with my name on it. Does the scumbag want to press charges?"

"Ha!"

"Then what?"

"Why?"

"Why what?"

"Why were you even there? Your mother tells me you haven't left your apartment since you quit therapy."

Xavier's hackles went up "My mother?"

"Don't get pissy, boy, she's worried; tells me you're not going home for Louise's wedding next month either."

"Why am I here, to talk about my mother?"

"No, it's just a side benefit to grill you; we will get to why you're here when we get to it. Now be a good Marine and answer."

Xavier tried to stare down the colonel but it was like trying to stare down a portrait, not going to happen. Both men let out a sigh when Xavier turned away. Xavier took a large drink from his spiked coffee. "I have been out, I go out every week whether I need to or not. I do laundry, take out the trash, and get beer," So what if he left out the part where it was in full combat fatigues with a weapon and two Xanax. Might not be a wise combination but it had been working since they sprang him from the loony bin.

"St. Cloud, you are stronger than this. You are one of the best men I known and that's saying something."

"Sir," Xavier said with a sigh.

"No, damn it, you piss me off, boy. You need to get over this pity party."

Xavier bolted out of the straight-backed wooden chair, toppling it over. "FUCK YOU AND THE HORSE YOU RODE IN

ON!" he shouted "You go watch your best friends die, you watch them be tortured because some dumb ass thought we knew where his fucking murdering, raping cronies were. 'Cause for some fucked up reason the ass thought we were CIA - we were in fucking fatigues but we were CIA. Bullshit, you can just drop dead," He was about to stalk out of the office, but the colonel was faster than he looked and he slapped a hand on the door.

"No, what's bullshit is this survivor's guilt you insist on living in. What's bullshit is you drinking your life away."

"You relive the worst day of your life every time you close your eyes, fuck, you guys don't get it. Oh, some of you older vets may think it's hard, but the friends you lost were from boot camp, not the fucking sand box or Goddamn preschool in a small town where EVERYONE KNOWS YOU. When you were the one to talk them into going into the Marines so we could get college money. When you were the one to talk them into special ops. Damn. Fuck," Xavier paced the office like an animal caged looking for the chink in the fence.

The colonel did know all of that; he also knew that Lance and Shawn had been lovers and were going to get out at the end of their tours and open a tattoo shop of all things. He knew what he was going to ask Xavier would either kill the boy or bring him back from the brink.

"Sit."

"No, damn it, I'm not a Marine anymore."

"Once a Marine, always a Marine!" the colonel yelled back.

Xavier wheeled around to face the man behind the desk. Before he could say a word, the colonel played the dirtiest card in the deck and simply said, "Semper Fidelis."

"Bastard," Xavier said heartlessly.

"Forever and always."

Xavier dropped back into the chair after righting it again. "Why am I here?" he asked in a whisper.

"Because, I have a task for you," Colonel Snyder said plainly.

"I'm out, get someone else."

"Can't, he's yours."

"I'm out," The younger man repeated.

"No, you're not, you've been on medical."

"Damn it, you said they wouldn't pull me back in!" Xavier shouted.

"They're not, I am."

CHAPTER FIVE

"Emiko, why on earth did you think you should take the deposit? Why on earth did you fight with him? He could have killed you. I have insurance for the deposit; the money can be replaced, but you can't!" Yvette shouted.

"I wanted to help, I wanted to be brave," Emiko whispered.

"I want you to be safe. That's what I want, that's all I want," Yvette answered.

"Yvette, I am not a child," though whispered her statement held strength.

"No, you're not, but you are also not street smart like Melissa or intimidating like me. And, well, Anne is just a charmer - they never bug her. Cassandra's, well let's face it chéri, she's a witch, there's no getting around it, she puts off a vibe that they can feel," Yvette patted Emiko's hand gently. "I'm not mad at you but you gave me a scare. I have never lost a chéri and I don't intend to start now. Emiko, please think about this... what would have happened to you if that man hadn't come, if he hadn't stopped the robber? You are so small the robber could have decided you were good enough to play with, to take home so to speak. Emiko, you know what the Yakuza do. We have people here who are just as mean," Yvette knew that would get though to her; the Japanese mafia had touched her family. Not as significantly, as Melissa had been by the American mob but the impression was still there.

She saw she had hit the mark as Emiko's shoulders began to shake. Glad that Cassandra wasn't there to have to undergo the barrage of emotions; Yvette pulled Emiko into an embrace. "I'm only telling you this so you will understand why I was so frightened when I heard what you had done. I don't handle being frightened well."

"I know," Emiko sniffled.

Yvette handed her a tissue. "So tell me about the man."

Emiko looked up in confusion. "The thief?"

"No, the man who rescued you."

"Oh, he, he was just there, saying something about it being a good idea for the man to leave me alone. The thief asked him who he thought he was. The man said he was a vet, too unstable to be left in combat."

Yvette cringed. '*Damn it, lady, you are supposed to give her someone to take care of her, someone to comfort her, not the other way around,*' she thought to herself, '*this better work out for the best.*'

Emiko continued to tell Yvette about Xavier and his odd behavior, while in the back of her mind she was trying to figure out something of her own - the strange feelings she had gotten when he had picked her up and carried her. She had never felt her stomach get so tight or so tingly before. Her skin was so raw and sensitive after he rubbed his thumb over it.

She was very baffled. Her heart had raced faster after her rescue than during her attack. She was so confused. "Yvette, can I ask a question?"

"Yes, chéri."

"Have you been robbed before?"

"Once, in New York, why?"

"Did your heart beat faster after?"

"No, well, for a few minutes after but mostly just while he had the knife pointed at me. I'll never forget him. He had a crescent shaped scar over his right eyebrow."

"Did he get away?"

"Yes, someone startled him but he still took my money."

"After the man knocked out the thief, he carried me back here. My heart raced more when he carried me than it did when the thief was threatening me."

Trying hard to keep a straight face Yvette said, "Really, what else?"

"My stomach was tight but it fluttered when he rubbed his thumb over my chin and it felt all tingly."

Yvette had to bite her cheeks not to laugh in the girl's face. Melissa, however, saved her from that. "Yvette, Stephanie wants to know when you're coming to meet the architect for the remodel. She says it's tomorrow or next month."

"Then it's next month, I have three four-hour long meetings tomorrow for new lines."

"Shouldn't you do lines after the remodel so you know when you can get them in?"

"Nope, because the remodel isn't for this store. It's for our new larger shop four stores down."

"What, wait, what are you talking about?" Melissa said confused. Emiko looked up in confusion as well.

"Magical Ways will be relocating in a few months. I figure just after Christmas. I'm thinking we will have a big Christmas/moving blow out sale. The new place has twice the retail and storage space and half again the office space."

"I thought you couldn't move because you had a ten year lease?"

"I do, but the owner said I could sub-let it so long as I didn't make a profit on the rent. I found a guy who wants to open a cigar store on the strip but the only place that fits size-wise is here. We met with the owner who happens to be a cigar connoisseur, and he liked the idea. Liam can't open until after the first of the year for supply reasons, so this works out well. The other shop doesn't need much in the way of structural changes; it's all cosmetic and ambiance. However, we can talk all about that later when all of us are here. I'll take you guys over next week when I get the keys. But let me tell the others, please."

"Yes," Emiko agreed. Melissa's fuchsia hair swaying as she nodded.

"Emiko, why don't you go home and rest? Come back tomorrow," Yvette nudged the girl.

"Are you sure?"

Yvette gave Emiko a look she knew the young girl would not argue with, "Very," It was strange that she had to use it now on the shy oriental. Emiko was always the one she never had to be stern with; she rather liked the change.

CHAPTER SIX

"You have got to be mother fucking kidding me. You want me to do what? No God damn way, not on your life, fuck. No not on my life, and that's what it would be, too."

"St. Cloud, you're over reacting."

"Like bloody hell I am."

"I want you to talk to the man-"

"In fucking Afghanistan!"

"Well yes, that is where he's being held," Snyder agreed.

"No," Xavier got up and walked to the door.

"Halt!" the colonel yelled.

"No!" Xavier shouted back even though he did as he was told.

"Once a Marine, always a Marine," Xavier heard again over his shoulder

"Damn it, old man, don't you understand what you're asking me?"

"Yes, I do."

"You want me to..."

"Question the man that brutally tortured you and your two friends for information you never had, and who ultimately ended up killing the friends who I know were lovers."

Spinning on his heel Xavier stammered, "What? How, no one…"

"A few did, no one chose to see it. As Marines, they were too good to throw out for stupid shit like that. I chose never to see it, what do I care who you sleep with? This is the home of the free and the brave."

"OoRah," Xavier mimicked the Marines' cry. "Colonel, why? Why me?"

"Reason A, because you deserve a shot at him. Reason B, because you *need* a shot at him. And Reason C, because getting to him may be just the ticket to getting yourself back. D, well reason D, because it's dangerous, and if you're going to do this crap," the colonel said throwing the file folder back at St. Cloud, "you should be getting paid for it."

Xavier shrugged his shoulders and flung the file back on the Colonel's desk. "I'll think about it. I take it he's someplace he'll keep?"

"Yes."

"Does anyone think he has current intel needed ASAP?"

"No," the colonel replied with a shake of his head.

"I'll let you know by the end of the week if I'll take it," Xavier walked out of the colonel's office slamming the door behind him. It felt good, kind of, like when he hung up on the old goat.

***

Half way back to his apartment it dawned on him he never got the present for Louise's wedding. "Fuck," he said aloud before he threw the Jeep into reverse and backed up the alley he used as a short cut to his complex.

He shouted, "Fuck!" again when he had to slam on the brakes to keep from hitting a cat. "Christ, a fucking black cat, what's next, a damned broken mirror?" Xavier waited for the cat to move out of his way and then backed the rest of the way out of the alley. Ten minutes later, he was in the same parking space he had been the day before. He got out and locked the Jeep, turned around and walked right into Emiko. He managed to catch her before she fell. "I'm so sorry. I should have been paying closer attention to where… oh it's you, trying to get mugged again?" Xavier said when he realized who it was.

"No, and I was not trying yesterday,"

"Looked like it to me."

"Then perhaps you need glasses."

"Ha."

Emiko had surprised herself; she never spoke like that to anyone. Yvette and Melissa teased her and tried to get her to tease back but she never did. It was bad manners and manners were everything in her family. Her family had a bond, but it was not like anything she had seen of her American friends. Their families were close: they touched, laughed, joked, and hugged. Hers did none of that. If there was any touching, it was only when necessary and always dignified. There also was no hanging around, no chillin' as Melissa called it. You were to be doing something useful at all times.

Xavier pulled Emiko out of her thoughts when he asked, "Why are you here again?"

"I am going home."

"Why?"

"Yvette sent me home for the day to let me rest and to think about how badly I reacted yesterday."

"What is she, your mother, sending you home from work like you're grounded?" asked Xavier, angry on Emiko's behalf.

"No, yesterday was very hard on me. I still have not told my parents; it was too late to call when I got home."

Xavier looked surprised. "How long did Sam keep you?"

"Only a moment or two after you, but it was very late in Japan."

"Wouldn't they want to know what had happened to you?"

Emiko turned away from the man; he looked as baffled as she felt. The odd feeling was back in her stomach. Briefly, she thought perhaps she should see a doctor.

"Wouldn't they?" Xavier pushed.

Emiko snapped out of her thoughts again at the sound of his voice. "No, they would not, my family is unhappy with me at this time."

"Why?" Xavier pressed again.

"I, I should not talk about it with you."

"What?"

Emiko shook her head, turned and began to walk home. When Xavier grabbed her arm, both of them jumped at the unexpected act and the reaction the touch caused.

"Sir, thank you for your help yesterday, but I am no longer need it," Emiko pulled her arm from Xavier and tried yet again to walk away but was still unsuccessful. Xavier pulled her into the alley they had been standing in front of, pressed her to the wall, and then startled them both by kissing her.

Emiko had never been kissed before, and certainly never like this. Being so surprised and overcome by sensations, she reacted on instinct. She mimicked everything Xavier did to her.

Emiko's response to him further inflamed Xavier; he stepped into Emiko, finding a perfect fit. This pushed him to the point of losing all common sense; his hands began to travel over Emiko's body her arms, her back, and butt. Emiko couldn't think, but somewhere the sounds of the world came back to her. She heard voices very close. This pulled her the rest of the way to reality. She shoved Xavier away, turned, and faced away from the street so no one would see her face.

Xavier, realizing what he had done, slammed his fist into the wall, cursing himself, and welcoming the pain. The pain replacing the lust. "Ma'am I'm sorry. I don't know what came over me. I don't go around kissing strangers in the alley, hell, most days I don't even leave my apartment. Please forgive me."

Emiko was confused; the twisted feeling was back but worse than ever before. "I told you I no longer needed your help. Please, just leave me alone."

"I will when you tell me you won't hate me."

"I cannot hate you. I do not know you. I do not even know your name."

"Xavier St. Cloud. It is a pleasure to meet you and you would be?"

"Emiko Nara."

Xavier caught Emiko off guard again by grabbing her hand, bowing, and then placing a kiss on her fingertips.

"My lady, I have committed a most egregious mistake upon your honor. Please allow me to correct this by permitting me to escort you to a lunch of your choosing."

Though Emiko understood what he was saying she was not sure why he was speaking like that. "You want to take me to lunch?"

"Yes, fair maiden. I would like get to know the woman who keeps me from my dark and humble abode."

"Why are you talking like that?"

"Forsooth because verily I have to think about it and if I am thinking of my words may haps I will not offend thee."

Emiko smiled a little and said, "Alright."

"So will you accept?"

Emiko thought for a moment but her stomach growled and she decided that as long as she was hungry she might as well eat. "Yes."

"Okay, where?"

"There is a very nice restaurant three blocks away."

"Good, lead the way," Xavier offered his arm, but Emiko declined and walked down the sidewalk on her own.

CHAPTER SEVEN

Emiko made it a little over a block before Xavier touched her shoulder. "Do you mind if we take a small detour? I need to stop at this store and buy a present for my sister. It's why I was here yesterday."

Emiko nodded and followed Xavier into MY SWEET DREAMS.

"Welcome to MY SWEET DREAMS, I'm Nick, how can I help you?"

"Um yeah, Ms. Thompson said to talk to you."

"Elderly lady in a BMW?"

"Yeah."

"We love Margret; she is one of our best customers."

"Okay."

"So do you know what you're looking for? A nice set of dishes for your first home?"

"What? No. No I'm looking for a wedding gift."

"Well, let me get you a scanner and you and your fiancé..." Xavier paled and looked at Emiko

"We're, no, we're not…"Xavier stuttered.

"Oh," Nick looked between the two.

"We are not engaged. The gift is for his sister," Emiko saw Xavier struggling and answered for him.

"Oh alright, what is her name and I will look up her registry list."

"She lives in Michigan," Xavier tried to explain.

"We have people who are registered with us from all over the world. They go online and add the items they want to their wish list, then family can buy the items and take them with them or we can ship them if the individual is unable to attend. I take it you can't get leave to attend?" Nick asked Xavier looking him up and down in his fatigues.

"Yeah, you could say that," Xavier answered, thinking about the colonel's offer. If he took it, it would be a while before he came back from Afghanistan, if he came back at all.

"What is her name?"

"Louisa St. Cloud."

"Okay," Nick walked to a computer and started typing. A moment later he turned and said "No, she is not registered with us, so let's try this: why did you come to MY SWEET DREAMS?"

"Margret said that it would be a good place to try because my sister liked to bake stuff, pastries and things."

"Alright, this way," Xavier followed Nick hoping the man would lead him to salvation so that he wouldn't have to go home. He flinched in anticipation of the pain he would feel if he were forced to go back and face his hometown.

"Do you know what she already has?"

Emiko watched Xavier turn even paler than before.

"I, uh, I don't know. I haven't seen her in about 2 years; we haven't really talked in five."

Nick faced Xavier. "Do you even know if she still likes to bake?"

"No," he whispered his answer.

"Perhaps you should talk to your sister before you buy her a gift."

Xavier walked out of the store without another word, leaving a baffled Emiko to apologize and to follow.

Once she caught up to him on the sidewalk outside, Xavier said, "I'm sorry, Emiko, let's just eat. I'll figure out what to do later. Where did you say the restaurant was?"

"A block or so," Emiko said pointing down one of the cross streets.

"Alright."

CHAPTER EIGHT

Emiko led him to a restaurant that she frequented whenever she was lonely and feeling homesick. When they entered, she spoke Japanese to the hostess, telling her that they wanted a private room and that they would like tea, then Saki. The girl led the way to a room in the back, opened a sliding rice paper door, and told Emiko that their server would be in soon with the tea.

"What was that all about?"

"I asked for a private room and for tea and Saki," she said. "The server will be here soon. Take your boots off," Emiko told him, pointing to his feet.

"Huh? Oh, yeah right," He sat down and began unlacing his combat boots. Emiko slid her small shoes off quickly and gracefully, then bent to help Xavier with his boots.

He noted the grace and sense of ease that he had not seen in her before. When they entered the room there was steaming tea set up on a table surrounded by pillows. Emiko knelt down on the far side of the table, Xavier sat down on her right side. He started to reach for the pot, but Emiko was already pouring the tea into his cup.

"May I ask a question?" Emiko asked softly.

"Yeah, I suppose."

"Why are you not going to your sister's wedding?"

"It's complicated and too dark to explain," he answered, hoping she would be too shy to push.

"Weddings are not dark."

"I know that's one of the reasons why I'm not going. There is a bunch of others."

"You are very confusing."

"I've had some rough times lately and seeing my family would just make it worse."

"And not talking to your sister for years is part of that?"

Xavier felt more trapped now than he ever had with the shrinks. At least they knew the basics; he only had to fill in the blanks. With Emiko, she knew nothing and he couldn't tell her.

"Maybe we should just order, though I can't read the menu."

"It is alright. I can, what do you like?"

"Just order two of everything you want."

Emiko spoke Japanese again when she ordered. Meanwhile Xavier kept trying to remember all the things that all of the therapists and shrinks had taught him when he started feeling overwhelmed. Flashes of Shawn and Lance worked through his mind, pictures of them trying to teach him some basic words in a few languages.

He reached for his tea to ease the dryness of his throat but caught a glimpse of how much his hands were shaking and thought better of it. "I need to use the rest room, where is it?" Xavier was happy that while his hands shook, his voice was steady.

"You should ask someone in the hall. I only know where the ladies room is, and I do not think it is near the men's room."

Jumping up quickly, he had to untangle himself from the pillows and the table. When he did, his shirt shifted so that Emiko could see a scar across his shoulder. *"I'm a Special Forces trained vet, they sent home for being too unstable to keep in combat,"* Xavier's words echoed in Emiko's mind, his sudden outburst made her wonder how unstable he was.

CHAPTER NINE

In the respite of the bathroom, Xavier fought for control of his inner demons. He leaned against the counter and counted repeatedly in his head, tired picturing an empty field, he said prayers, demanded he straighten out, pleaded with himself to be the way he used to be, and then berated himself when he jumped as another patron came in. The man only briefly looked in Xavier's direction and continued with his business. Xavier washed cold sweat from his hands with even colder water, then left to face Emiko.

Emiko was on the verge of panicing when Xavier finally returned; he had been gone for nearly ten minutes. She was about to go looking for him when he reappeared behind their server with the food and Saki. The server waited for Xavier to sit down before serving.

The small waitress only made Xavier that much more nervous. He took a drink of his tea praying his hands wouldn't betray him.

How in the hell was he supposed to interrogate a mid-level Taliban leader if the idea of a serving girl being in arm's reach made him tremble and jump? There was no way he could do it; he'd probably wet himself before he got through the door. He would have to call the colonel and do the hardest thing in his life - turn down a mission he had been ordered to go on. He was sure he would crumble before he got to the airport.

Emiko watched Xavier; his face was, to her, an open book, his emotions showing clearly. People had sometimes wondered if she was like was an empath like Cassandra. She wasn't empathic, she didn't feel the emotions of others, but she saw them. Maybe it was because of her upbringing, she had been raised to anticipate her future husband's smallest needs and wishes…to know what he wanted before he knew he wanted it.

Emiko saw in the face of the man across from her fear, frustration, anger, loss, confusion, and something she had no experience with and couldn't place, desire. After their waitress left, Xavier looked questioningly at her, "What did you order?"

At least now, she understood one of the emotions: he had no idea what was on the plate in front of him. "I was expecting rice and brown meat."

"You were expecting teriyaki."

"Yeah, I guess."

"The little plate is sushi. There are some California rolls and some spring rolls. No raw fish, just rice, seaweed, and some vegetables. The seaweed does have a strong taste to it. The green ball is Wasabi. It is very hot, and no, it is not like Hispanic hot, it is worse. No matter how many habanera peppers you eat, this is nothing like that. The yellow paste is mustard, it is warm, but it is mild compared to the Wasabi. I also ordered Yaki Udon, which is just chicken, and noodles and a few vegetables."

"Um, yeah, okay," Xavier tried one of the California rolls; he was startled by the strong fish flavor but liked it all the same. Then he tried the second roll and decided it was also good but the first was better. Emiko had started on the noodle bowl. Xavier realized that there were no

American utensils on the table. "Um, uh, I, um, I've never used chopsticks before. Would it be bad manners to ask for a fork?"

"No, I will get you one," A moment later, she had a fork and a spoon.

Xavier looked at both thankfully. He really wished he could just have the teriyaki chicken he was used to, but he tried the noodles tentatively. When he took the first bite, he decided that maybe he should be a little more adventurous because it was good.

On the other side of the table, Emiko was trying to get the courage to ask him about the scar, but her upbringing had taught her from a very young age not to ask such things.

Xavier was trying to calm his mind, so he decided to distract himself by asking Emiko questions, "What do you do at the shop, besides trying to get mugged?"

"Almost mugged," she said quietly.

"Right, almost."

"I help the customers, I run the register. Yvette was very kind to give me this job. I have never worked before."

"Never worked in a clothing shop you mean?" he said thinking he had missed something.

"No, I had never worked anywhere before. In my family, we do not work."

"All of your family?" he questioned.

"No, the women. We do not work. Only the men work. My family owns a large trading company, Nara Trading. It has been passed from father to son for three hundred years. The sons are trained from a very young age for the responsibility of being a Nara, and what they will be doing in the company. The girls are taught at young age that we will be perfect wives, learning our husbands so they will have no need to ask for anything. A wife must know before a husband what he needs so it can be waiting for him to reach for it."

"Are your lives are planned out for you? What if you want to be a doctor or hell, a fire fighter or sail boats?"

"You can sail boats on your vacations and no one has wanted to be a fire fighter."

"What about a doctor?" Xavier pushed.

"No, not that either."

"Wait, now if no women in your family work, why are you working, and in the States no less?"

Emiko shifted uncomfortably on her pillows. "My betrothed left me," she whispered.

"What? Wait, they still do betrothals?" Xavier exclaimed in disbelief.

"Yes."

"So what does that have to do with you being in the States?" Xavier demanded.

Emiko took a bite of her noodles but instead of the soft rice flour noodles, she felt as if she had taken a bite of sand. She could barley swallow it; she tried to wash it down with her tea, but that only made it worse since she managed to scald her mouth.

"Emiko, are you ok?" Xavier saw her struggle with the bite of noodle, and then burn her throat. He handed her his glass of ice water.

"Calm down, are you okay?"

Nodding and taking a deep breath, "Yes, I am alright."

"I didn't mean to pry, trust me, that is the last thing I wanted to do. I've had enough people do it to me."

Stalling, Emiko drank the ice water; hoping he would change the subject so that she would not have to tell him. Melissa had told her more than once that the shame was her family's and her betrothed's, not hers. However, a man may see things differently than a woman. Emiko could tell he was hoping for an answer but would not press. "May we talk about something else? I, it, I, oh, it is hard to explain outside of my family."

"I suppose," Xavier granted her wish and let the subject drop, but hoped that she would confide in him one day.

They ate the rest of the meal in an awkward silence, neither wanting to push the other more than they had already been pushed. Xavier thought maybe he should try to talk to that shrink Sam had mentioned, someone not paid by Uncle Sam. Maybe he would have some way of helping. However, the next thought was that whoever it was would need security clearance because of the type of ops

Xavier had been on when everything happened.

"*Fuck, one step forward, three steps back*," he thought to himself.

Emiko looked up at Xavier. They made eye contact for a moment, but when he smiled, she ducked her head back down, her stomach clenching and rolling again. Her stomach kept reacting to him. She just did not understand this. However, she was twenty-five and felt embarrassed to ask someone what it meant.

On the other side of the table Xavier wasn't faring much better; he felt damaged and undeserving of anything as pure as Emiko seemed. He had felt tainted since Afghanistan.

When he was in high school, he had wanted a family: wife, kids, floppy-eared dog to bark at nothing and play a mean game of tug of war. He had let the dream go on the third day of his capture, knowing for certain he was never going to see the light of day again.

Then when Lance and Shawn died, he gave up all hope, none of which returned when he woke up in the ICU. His commander was telling him that it wasn't a dream, they were dead, and he wasn't. The guilt he felt was and is killing him.

In high school, his nickname had been "Saver" for more than one reason. He had become a volunteer in the local fire department. It was a small town, so all the emergency services were on an on-call basis. He had trained on his own time to become an EMT and received his certification, the youngest person ever in the county.

Soon after that, he was on a call and through a smoke-fogged window of a crappy little trailer being using as a meth lab, until it exploded, he saw a fire fighter trapped by fallen debris. The fireman's coat had been caught on something, the fireman's PASS – Personal Alert Safety System - hadn't gone off yet, so no one knew he was in trouble.

Later the fire chief asked him what the hell he thought he was doing. He told the chief he didn't think, just reacted. The chief laughed and called him the Saver's Saver, the name stuck.

When Lance, Shawn, and Xavier all joined the Corps, everyone in town was surprised. The town knew they would go into the military for the college money, but they had expected it to be one with a medical service, which the Marine Corps lacks. They relied on their "sister services" for that and any religious needs. There was some basic first aid taught, but for the most part, if a Marine was hurt too far from help, he was going to die depending on the wound.

Savers' knowledge had come in handy during his first op. One of the guys in his unit broke his leg, Saver set it, and the man was able to hobble out of the forest on some makeshift crutches on his own. The army doctors had credited Saver with the man being able to walk without a limp. But after his friends died, no one but Sam had called him Saver.

The silence between Emiko and Xavier was nearing critical mass, when their waitress came in to ask if they would like anything else, but both of them said no at the same time so she left and returned a moment later with the check. Xavier took it from her before she set it down.

"I will pay. It was my idea to come here," Emiko whispered.

"No, I will because, well, because I said so."

Emiko did not argue; it simply wasn't in her make up to argue, yet.

Xavier crossed to Emiko's side of the table to help her from the cushions but misjudged how light she was and pulled her right into this chest.

"I oh, I oh," the funny feeling was back. Her stomach pitched and rolled and her skin felt as if she had stepped into a fire. She barely had time to adjust to that feeling when Xavier growled and pulled her face toward his. The feeling intensified when his lips met hers. The kiss in the alley was nothing compared to the raw desire and sheer lust of this kiss.

Her fiancée had certainly never tried to kiss her; he had never cared enough to show her any affection. Emiko moaned at all of the new sensations flowing through her. Emiko leaned into Xavier after a moment. Her legs were weak and she did not feel steady on them.

Xavier felt her shift and it was enough to bring him out of his haze. "Damn it," he pulled back from Emiko and looked down at her face. She looked moony-eyed and lost. Her features were cast perfectly; he thought that she must have been made in the image of some Japanese goddess. She was too beautiful to be common.

"Did I...did I do..."

Guessing at what she was trying to say, Xavier said, "No, Emiko, you didn't do anything wrong. You are perfect, but I would bet my left hand that you have never been kissed by anyone but me."

"I did do something wrong," Emiko whispered dropping her head in shame.

Lifting her shin and looking in her eyes, "No, you didn't, but I'm not going to make out with you in a damned restaurant. We don't know each other and, while that's not required for kissing, it does help because very often kissing leads to other things that do require knowing the other person," Xavier tucked her arm under his and walked her to a public area before he lost his will power again and kissed her. "Where is your car?"

"I do not drive. I only live a few blocks away."

"You can't walk home."

"I do every day. Melissa drives me sometimes, but mostly I walk."

"Don't you know how dangerous it can be out there? No, you don't or you wouldn't have almost gotten mugged because you would have taken a taxi to the bank," Xavier was about to hail her a taxi when her cell rang.

Pulling her phone from her pocket she answered, "Konnichiwa."

Xavier saw her face pale and her skin flush simultaneously as a stream of Japanese came though her tiny little phone.

"Okasan..." More rapid Japanese interrupted whatever Emiko had hoped to say. Tears slid down her cheeks. "Mama, no," Emiko shook her head.

"*She's crumbling,*" he thought. He'd never seen it before but he figured whatever her mother was saying in Japan would destroy her world in America. Never able to stand seeing anyone in pain, Xavier snatched the phone from Emiko and said, "Whatever you just told your daughter made her cry. From what little I understand, this isn't the first time but it will be the last time if I can do anything about it," He snapped the neon pink phone closed and dropped it in an astonished Emiko's coat pocket. Before the shock could wear off, he hailed her a cab, got her address from her and handed the cabby a twenty for a three-dollar fare.

The yellow car was gone before Xavier's adrenaline wore off and he realized he had no clue how to get back to his Jeep.

CHAPTER TEN

"Saver, twice in two days. It's a new record."

But Xavier rounded on Sam before he could stop himself, he did manage to pull back the punch, but the other man was pinned to the wall. "Down boy, down," Sam said in a flat tone with deadpan eyes, cop's eyes that saw death and wanted to show it no fear.

"Fuck," Xavier stalked off towards a partially obscured part of the alley. He kicked the dumpster, hit it, and then turned around and leaned his head on the brick wall.

Sam straightened his collar and followed Xavier. "Man, you have got to get help; you have to get this under control."

"I've tried."

"Try again, you're going to end up killing someone, and that will finish you off."

"Who? I can't talk about it to just anyone; what happened is above classified."

Sam took out his pen from his pocket and grabbed Xavier's hand. He scribbled a number on it and ordered, "Use it. He had clearance, and he's not paid by the government. I've told him what little I know. He's waiting for you."

"I don't know, Sam, it's been so long," Xavier whispered hoarsely. "Am I still in here somewhere?"

"Yes, because you stopped yourself from pounding me just now."

Xavier scrubbed his face, and then ran a hand through his hair. "Sam, I can't. I don't...I don't know if I can go through Lance and Shawn again."

"Xavier, you go through it every day. You need to be able to *not* go through it, and you need to be able to close the door or at least pull a damn curtain. I don't want your name to be on either of the boards at the station," Sam told him referring to the suspect/victim boards some departments used to try to solve crimes. "Look, I'm off the rest of the day. Let me take you over to Max, and at least meet him."

Xavier shrugged, "Got nothing else to do," so he followed Sam out of the alley over to his old beat up two-tone brown GMC Jimmy. "When are you going to get a new ride?" Sam had been driving the old thing when Xavier had been in high school with Sam's daughter.

Sam laughed and said, "When I don't have kids in braces or college."

"So never?"

"Pretty much."

They rode in silence to the other side of town. Xavier tried not to think about the things he might have to discuss with Max. However, when he wasn't thinking about Afghanistan, he was thinking about Emiko, and thinking of her only managed to tie him into bigger knots. It surprised him that she scared him more than his internal war. Then there were thoughts of what the colonel wanted from him, he wondered again if he would ever be whole. A few minutes later Sam pulled in front of a storefront. "Thought we were going to a head shrinker?"

"We are. His wife has a new age shop. She's been hassled a bit, so he's working out of her shop for a while."

"Looking out for her?"

"Yeah, or as he puts it 'waiting to trounce the little shits who keep making my girl cry'."

Images of Emiko in tears came to Xavier, as did his statement to her mother. He shouldn't have said that, but in his entire life, he had never backed down from a promise.

Sam walked into the shop. "Max, you in here?"

"Maxwell is out back, pretending to break down my boxes, so he can pollute his lungs with chemicals."

"Hi, Crystal," Sam nodded in the direction of the voice, "Xavier and I will go find him and rough him up for you."

"Thank you, Samuel."

Xavier raised an eyebrow "Samuel?"

"Well, what did you think my first name was?"

"Samuel, just didn't think anyone used it."

"Only Crystal, she uses everyone's full first name. No nicknames with her."

"Sam, good to see you," said a man about six feet tall with a little salt in his short-cropped black hair, and he extended his hand toward Sam.

Taking the offered hand Sam said, "Crystal's on to your ploy, old man."

"Damn it. It's hell living with a nature lover."

"Um, as a doctor shouldn't you know those are bad for you?" Xavier questioned pointing towards the cigarette.

"Sure, but if everyone did only what was good for them and those around them, you two would be out of jobs and mine would be a part time one. Xavier, I presume," Max said reaching his hand out.

"Yeah, how…"

"You're all Marine, you exude the Marine pheromone, and anyone with previous experience with the military would be able to spot it."

Xavier didn't know if he liked being spotted so easily or not but accepted it for what it was: the truth.

"Look, I understand you're probably a little gun shy, so to speak, about talking to yet another shrink. Another busybody poking around in your head, but I think if we can try to get to know one another on a casual level, then maybe you will be able to deal a little better with what happens when it is time to talk."

"Well, it's an approach no one else has tried. Maybe."

"Good. Barbeque, my place, this weekend. Sam will pick you up, ten sharp," Max said gruffly.

"Ten's early for a barbeque," Xavier said

"Not at their place. Chateau de Salitine is 40 miles outside of town."

"What's your poison?" the shrink asked.

"Any beer," Xavier replied.

" 'K, see you there."

"Later Max," Sam turned and pushed Xavier ahead of him.

"Bye Crystal, see you this weekend."

"Flesh eater!" the petite blond responded.

"Yep."

"Vegetarian I take it?" Xavier asked.

"Oh yeah, but I've seen her sneak a bite of Max's steak every once in a while."

"So, Samuel, how much have you told Maxwell?" he asked the cop, picking on him for the name.

Ignoring the jab, Sam answered, "I don't know much. I've told him what I do know, though. Look I need a beer," Sam pulled in front of a local cop bar. "Let's get a pint," The two men walked into the bar and the bartender looked at the clock, "Day off?"

"Yeah, Brodey," Sam said holding two fingers up.

" 'K."

"Come here a lot, I take it?" Xavier asked.

"Couple times a week. Susan takes sewing and cooking classes so I come here."

"Ah."

A few minutes later Sam said, "Thanks, Brodey."

"Tab?" asked the bushy bearded bartender as he set down the two glasses of beer in front of the men.

"Yeah, catch you Friday?" Sam said picking up the pint of Guinness.

"Right," Brodey nodded as he wandered back to the bar.

"Look, Xavier, most people figured out about Lance and Shawn, but no one wanted to, well, kill their careers, so no one let on that they were lovers. We all had an idea what you guys did in the corps, but no one knew for sure, no what's or where's, no details. We could put things together, though."

"We knew everyone got that we were special ops, but we figured they hid the relationship enough."

"No, not really," Sam shook his head.

"I wish I could tell you about it. The three of us were good. Lance and Shawn could blend into any group; I had a little harder time. We played it like they were my guides or something," Xavier drank heavily from his Guinness, his training fighting with his brain's attempt at self-preservation. "Fuck this crap. I need someone to know and it needs to be you. We...we were in Afghanistan, Lance and Shawn were in as mid-level officials. We were supposed to bait this sleeper cell into coming to us. Then we could capture and turn that group, get as many as we could to talk and get more and so on."

"Okay, so what happened?" Sam wondered.

"One of the newer recruits had seen us six months before on an op in Rumalia, Iraq. Nothing big but he knew we weren't locals."

"Shit, blown before it was planned," Sam muttered.

"Yeah, no way we could have known either," Xavier replied with regret.

"So when you tell this to the shrinks..."

"They go into how there was nothing I could have done, almost died myself, yada yada."

"You did."

"I know, but I should have died. Look, I watched the bastard beat and torture them; they took turns doping us with speed or something while the others were..." Xavier downed the rest of his beer and signaled for another.

"I get it," Sam offered, hoping his young friend wouldn't have to go through the entire hell he had lived though.

Xavier downed half of the second beer as soon as Brodey set it down. He missed the head tip from Brodey in his direction as well as the headshake from Sam telling him not to worry. Rubbing his hand over his face, Xavier tried to push down the heart-pounding anxiety that came with talking about what happened.

"Xavier, you survived the un-survivable. There is a reason for that, you are meant to go on and do something."

"I know. I get that, but something…damn it, fuck, Sam. I watched, chained to the damn ceiling, as he took my fucking gun, stuck it in Lance's mouth, and blew his brains all over Shawn. I saw the devastation in his eyes as Shawn realized what had just happened. The son of a bitch had kept us for two weeks. You guys knew they were lovers. He didn't get it, all the torturing he had done, he never got that they wouldn't look at each other when they were up. Then I had to watch him take that same gun, the one I carried, fucking hell, still carry and put it to Shawn's temple and see his brains on the wall. The guy had finally figured we weren't going to tell him anything after this long, so no need to waste time or supplies on us. He turned to me and I knew my number was up."

"Wait! How the hell did you?" Sam asked confused.

"Damn Taliban."

"Wait, what, I have Bin Laden to thank for only two funerals?"

"In a roundabout way, yeah. Someone hit the complex with small missiles. Knocked jackass off his feet, but the bullet that was supposed to kill me lodged in my shoulder," Sam watched as Xavier absently reached where the scar must be from the bullet. "Everyone escaped in the confusion but they left me hanging. Figured I was toast, was just going to take longer and be more painful. Found out that the ass who had us was a minor leader who had pissed off the wrong bigger leader."

" 'K," Sam said astonished and waited to see if Xavier would finish.

"Five hours, give or take, and an allied patrol checking the area because of the explosion found me and realized I was no local."

"Gee I wonder why?" Raising a eyebrow, Sam said sarcastically.

"I was babbling, they got that I was American, took me to an Allied base from there. I was patched up and traveled to Ramstein Air Base in Germany, and I finally woke up there some two weeks later," Pausing to drain the second half of his beer and signal for a third, he continued. "Most of it I had blocked out but the powers that be figured out enough because the patrol brought Lance and Shawn's bodies back, too."

"So why didn't talking to the docs help?"

"I couldn't tell them the whole story," Xavier said with a shrug.

"Lance's and Shawn's records would be fucked, one for being gay and two for being a gay couple working together?"

"Right."

"So to save two dead friends' reputations, you have been losing your sanity and I might add tearing your family's and friends' lives apart, tearing these people's hearts out, and tramping on them."

"Would you turn in a dead bad cop killed in the line of duty doing good?"

Sam started to answer and drew up short. Would he? The cop's family would get zero and a bad reputation. Lance's and Shawn's families would get the same, and all the ops they had gone on trying to make the world a better place would mean nothing because they would be out, dishonorably discharged, dead or alive, for being gay.

"No, I wouldn't. But I also wouldn't turn myself inside out over it either," Sam stated.

Xavier snorted and answered, "No, only I do stuff like that."

"Xavier, you know if it had gone any other way you would be dead, too. If you had played hero they would have shot you first and then Lance and Shawn. There would have been memorials instead of funerals because there would have been no bodies found."

Xavier knew all of this, had heard all of it before. It still didn't help. He knew there was nothing he could have done then to change what happened, but it still hurt, and that was what he couldn't get past.

Sam watched Xavier go into his own world and he figured he was going though some, if not all of the tragedy. He didn't know if he should try to pull him out of it or not, but the door slammed behind them, and the choice was gone. Xavier jumped and cursed. Sam chuckled, "Least you didn't take a swing at me again; might have a hard time explaining that to the crew around here."

Xavier glanced around seeing that the whole place was full of cops both in and out of uniform. He found all the under covers quickly enough. They dressed as if they didn't belong, but their carriage and mannerisms gave them away immediately. He shook his head, looked at Sam and said, "Before I would have known exactly how many people were in this room, how many had gone to the john and how many times, could tell you who's cheating and with whom most likely, if they were in the room, too. Plus I would have a good chance at telling how many were dirty. Now, fuck, when we came in it was the bartender and us, and one guy in the back...I never saw them come in. I can't do it, can't do what he wants," Xavier finished his monologue muttering to himself.

Sam caught part of it but figured Xavier had broken enough rules today, he wouldn't push the man any further. "Look, you have to try something. I realize that I'm not the best person for you to dump on, but I am here."

"I know. Look, just take me to my Jeep, would ya? I gotta, I've got to go," Since noticing the number of people in the room, Xavier's anxiety level had steadily gone up, and he was almost at his limit.

"Sure, man, no problem. Where are you parked?"

"Near Magical Ways."

Sam looked at Xavier questioningly. "Trying to get beat up again?"

"No, I wasn't. I was getting a present yesterday for Louise's wedding. Then when everything went down I forgot, so I went back."

"But that's not where I found you."

"Yeah, I ran into that girl again," Xavier explained.

"Emiko?"

"Yeah, I was rude."

"Surprise," Sam joked.

"Yeah, ha. Anyway..."

"You were rude," Sam restated.

"Yeah, and I, God, I kissed her twice," Xavier said confused.

"You kissed her?" Sam asked with a raised eyebrow.

"Shhhhh, damn it, keep your voice down," Xavier looked around the room after Sam's outburst. Only a few people had even looked in their direction.

"Xavier, for Christ's sake, this is not some op where secrecy is vital. Hey everyone! My friend here is an ex-spook and he kissed a girl today!"

"Get a room," The room broke out in laughter and well wishes, a few of which were actually repeatable. Xavier shoved out of the booth and threw a wad of bills on the table, "I'll find the Jeep myself."

Sam scrambled out behind him. "Damn it, stop."

"No!" The angry Marine yelled over his shoulder.

"Yes! You're too young, too tall and I'm too old, too short."

"Damn it, Sam, look I..."

"Xavier, look man, it was a joke. No one in that place gives a damn about anything. They are off work, away from the desk, the beat, the hell, the captain, the whatever. But what's said in that place stays there. Who are they gonna tell? It's a cop bar, not someplace that your spook-type cover is going to get blown."

"I don't have a spook-type cover. I was never a spook; I was just in special ops."

"Still are," Colonel Snyder said behind Xavier. He didn't receive the reaction he was expecting.

"Drop dead. TAXI!" Xavier yelled, flagging down the yellow car.

"Sergeant St. Cloud."

"No," and with that, Xavier was gone in the back of a taxi.

"Now why is it, when I want one of those I can never find one and when I don't they're everywhere?" Sam asked absently.

"Same with cops," the colonel replied.

"Might want to be careful with that one, you are standing in front of the local blue line pub."

"So I see," the colonel replied.

"So how do you know Saver?"

"I know Sergeant St. Cloud because he is under my command."

"Hmmm, I see," Seconds later the colonel was backpedaling to get his balance after Sam punched him.

CHAPTER ELEVEN

"Listen here you jackass, you fucked up a good kid and got two others killed."

"No, I did not. They were not under my command before the incident. I only got Xavier afterwards, and I am doing what I can to help the boy get himself back. He just doesn't see it that way right now."

"Really, and how do you think you're helping him? Best I get is that he hasn't left his apartment for months," Sam mentioned.

"Hm, well, I know that he did yesterday."

"Yeah, he did. I was the one who got the call to investigate it."

"Ah, are you Sam or Tom?"

"Sam," Sam said cautiously.

"Ah, good, glad to meet you," Snyder offered his hand.

"Glad you know who I am; who the hell are you?" Sam accepted the offered hand.

"Colonel Sydney Snyder, Commander of Special Operations, Ft. Stein."

"Nice title," Sam said, sarcasm dripping from the two words.

Snyder countered with, "Yes, well, I did not have it three years ago."

"I'll let two good boys slide for you then."

"I wish there was something I could say to help him but there isn't, and what he has to do to get past it will hurt as much as the original break."

"That's twice you've said something cryptic that."

"Yes."

"Look, I don't care for all this cloak and dagger crap. I know enough to know that those boys shouldn't have been where they were and shouldn't have been left to die. If you think you're sending him back out into that kind of crap, you better think again, because there is no way he can handle it!" Sam yelled.

"Well, I think what I have in mind will help," Snyder said calmly, "I have a call into the boy's therapist first, to see what he thinks, but I have a feeling he will agree with me."

"Because he's army paid?"

"I'm sorry?" Snyder asked not understanding Sam.

"He'll agree because he's paid by the government, right?"

"No, actually he's an independent fellow," the colonel answered off-hand.

"Hot damn, Max does move fast," Sam said, slapping the colonel in the arm.

"Yes, Maxwell is his first name. He asked for Xavier's file today; I just okayed it. I take it you know Maxwell Salitine."

"Yeah, I know Max and his wife; I've known them for years actually. Xavier isn't the only black ops guy I know, nor will he be the last, I'm sure. I asked Max a few months ago if he would see Xavier, if I could get him to agree to come in, and Max said yes. I saw Xavier for the first time in quite a while yesterday. I was going to head to his place today to talk to him about it, especially after what happened, but I saw him, more or less, lost not far from little Tokyo, and well, he would have laid me out if he hadn't recognized me."

"Damn boy's going to kill someone."

"Most likely. I talked him into meeting Max."

"Happen to know how it went? Damn, probably not – patient-doctor crap?"

"Um, actually I do. I'm taking him to Max's Saturday for a barbeque."

"Excuse me?" the confused colonel asked.

"Max's technique is different. He figures there's a reason best friends know all the good juicy gossip. All his barbeques are for patients to get comfortable and chummy, so to speak."

"I don't know if that is…"

The cop interrupted the officer to say, "It is the best thing for Xavier."

"So you're a therapist?"

"No, I've known Xavier for years; knew Lance and Shawn, too. They went to school with my oldest daughter. For a while we all thought maybe Lisa and Lance would get together because, well, they were always together."

"I don't know if you know this…"

"That Lance and Shawn were lovers?" Sam finished "Yeah we all got that later, you were the guys who weren't supposed to know."

"Those boys couldn't keep it a secret from what I understand. They showed it every time they looked at each other. I met them but separately."

"Hey look, wait, why were you here anyway?" Sam asked.

"My sister works just down the block. We were supposed to meet for drinks. On my way, I saw Sergeant St Cloud."

"He's out, so how about Xavier?"

"No, actually he's not."

"Not what, out?" Sam was once again confused.

"Yes, he is still in the reserves; he's been on medical leave since waking."

"You bastard, you're pulling him back in. You want him whole so you can use him again for your shit," Sam ranted.

"No, for his own good."

"Come again?"

"Xavier needs this last mission. It can't right all the wrongs but if he can survive it - and he can - it will bring him back from this."

"You gonna stake his life on it?" Sam demanded.

"I am."

Sam wondered aloud, "So what do you know that I don't?"

"In this matter, everything."

Cryptically Sam said, "Don't bet on that."

"He...did he? He did not tell you." The colonel stammered.

"Some of it. Look Xavier is a walking time bomb. When, not if, when he goes off, if he doesn't kill himself, whatever he does will. He needed someone to talk to. Yes, he will talk to Max, but to keep him sane today, he needed to talk to me. I would never tell anyone what he told me. Besides, he didn't give me any mission details. The only thing he told me was about Lance and Shawn being shot."

"He shouldn't have told you that much, but given the situation, we will overlook it."

Sarcasm returning to Sam's voice again, "Magnanimous of you. We need to make sure he gets help and soon...someone should have been nudging him along the whole time. As his friends and superior, we have all failed him."

"If only I could refute that."

***

As Sam and the colonel were debating their standing as friends with Xavier, he was at the liquor store buying Jim Beam Black. If it had been the new girl, he'd seen last month he would have just bought a damn case but it was the old lady he saw last week when he had bought three bottles, he opted for the three again with the lame excuse of poker night. She just looked at him shook her head and rang him up. Xavier knew he was busted but didn't care; he didn't want to be conscious for the next forty-eight hours and if he spent them all drunk with no memory of those forty-eight, so be it.

CHAPTER TWELVE

Emiko sat on her bed crying. She was sure that at anytime her father would knock on her door to take her back to Japan and her parents' home, to take her away from the life she had been building here. She was sure that her mother would find her an acceptable husband for her to marry, whether she wanted to or not. The wishes of the Nara children had never been taken into consideration. No child had ever rebelled...no one had ever even thought to rebel.

Yvette stood outside Emiko's door debating with herself over whether she should knock or not. Yvette knew the girl's parents had called. They had called the shop to talk to her there. Yvette was unsure why they had called the store instead of her cell.

She might know some things, but damn it, she was not omnipotent and most days she was glad of it. Today, however, was not one of those days. She had barely had the chance to say that Emiko wasn't in before the line went dead. Being hung up on was not something Yvette took well.

Having a bad feeling about what the Nara's had planned for their daughter, Yvette left Anne at the shop to close. She left instructions to leave the deposit in the new safe and that she would take care of it tomorrow. She walked the dozen or so blocks to Emiko's apartment, which she shared with two other girls who came from the same region in Japan as Emiko.

Yvette knocked on the door, deciding that she needed to know what had been done so she could fix it.

Emiko didn't hear the knock at first, lost in her own grief over what her mother had said on the phone. When the knock turned into pounding, Emiko jumped with a start. In her broken heart she knew it was her father there to take her back; her mind knew that an hour ago he had been yelling in the background when her mother had called and that there was no way he could have made the trip half way across the world in an hour. Finally, through the fog she heard Yvette call out her name in fear.

"Emiko! Emiko! Open this door!" Yvette knew something had to be wrong. Emiko would never let someone stand at her door for this long, but Yvette had already tried the door, and it was locked. She wished for Melissa; the girl knew ropes and locks. "Emiko! You better open this door before I call the police!" Yvette finished as the door opened to reveal a frightened and sobbing Emiko.

"Oh gods, baby, what did they do to you this time?" Yvette asked, now on the inside of the door. Emiko was so pale that she looked as white as Melissa did and with her heritage, that was indeed a feat. Yvette led Emiko to the couch and sat her down; the girl seemed to crumple in on herself, falling over to her side sobbing harder.

Yvette left her to find the kitchen, knowing there had to be tea somewhere in the apartment. Finding some already made but cool she put it in the microwave for a few seconds and, after checking the temperature, she took the cup to Emiko.

"Baby, chéri, darling, I need you to sit up chéri a aimé, sit up," Yvette continued to coax the girl until she finally did, and Yvette helped her to drink the tea.

The sobs finally faded, and Emiko curled into Yvette's lap. Now that the sobbing was done Yvette could feel the girl shaking, and whether it was with fear over what would happen or with fatigue from the crying, Yvette was about to find out.

"Emiko a aimé, what did your mama say to you? I know she called you," Emiko stiffened and curled in tighter on herself again. "A aimé, tell me chéri, I will fix it."

"No, no, they are coming. They are coming to take me back."

"They cannot take you to Japan unless you let them, chéri. Even though they are your parents, you are an adult. They may demand, threaten or whatever they want, but they *cannot* take you anywhere."

Yvette felt Emiko relax millimeter by millimeter; she began rubbing the girl's arm. "You're staying here on a work visa that I helped you get. They cannot change that. You are here because you want to be here, and we want you to be here. You do so much for us Emiko; we need you."

"I do nothing."

"Yes, you do, a aimé. You are our little sister, our littlest sister. You are the one that we all need to be able to look out for. Cassandra needs to be able to draw from your stillness when we all get to be too much for her. Melissa needs you to remember that there are still innocents in the world. She needs to know that life does have rainbows in it. You are her rainbow. Anne needs you to baby. She has never gotten the bébé she deserves, so you are the one she takes care of and worries over, fawns over and does what needs to be done. And I need you peu qu'un, much as Cassandra needs you; I need you because you remind me that there is a still place in the world. When I need to meditate, I think of how calm you are, how graceful you are, and I think of you: how like a reed, you bend, but you do not break."

"I break."

"No chéri, you bend very far, but you do not break."

"I was broken when you came."

"You were cracked, not broken. You are fine my dear; oh my chéri, you are fine."

Yvette smoothed the girl's hair down, combing out some of the tangles with her fingers. "Now, do you want to go back to Japan?" Yvette refused to call it home...home was here with her family by choice, not blood.

"No," Emiko said so quietly Yvette strained to hear the single word.

"Then don't."

"But my father..."

"Can get his useless, undeserving ass back on the plane and fly home."

Emiko sat up straight when she heard Xavier's voice speak from her front door.

"My father..."

"Does not deserve you, chéri," Yvette agreed with the man in the doorway. She was sure this was the man who saved Emiko. Patting the girl's leg, she walked over to him and introduced herself, "Yvette Lacroix. Thank you for saving my peu qu'un."

"You're what?"

"My little one."

"Ah," Xavier did not like the scrutiny he was getting from this woman.

Yvette shook Xavier's hand, felt the small tremor and smelled a mild trace of Jim Beam. *'He better not be an alcoholic, lady, I will hurt you for that,'* she thought.

"I cannot send my father away when he comes," Emiko spoke from the couch; both people turned and watched the girl as if she had grown horns. Emiko did her best not to squirm or fidget under both angry glares.

"Then you don't; one of us will," Xavier stated as if that had been the plan all along.

"I think that would be a very good idea," Yvette found herself agreeing with the solider again.

"No, I... "Emiko started to say something, but it was lost when the twin glares started again.

"You will go into your room and get clothes and you will go to Anne's and stay until we get your father on the right track; your mother, too for that matter. You have had enough stress for a year, let alone for a few days. Melissa would be better in case your father tries to force the matter, but her couch is so bloody uncomfortable that I wouldn't curse anyone with that thing."

Turning toward the desk, Xavier wrote a number down and handed it to Yvette. "If he should try, call this number. Sam will be there with everyone he can pull on short notice. And as long as Sam has been on the force here, that is a large number of cops."

"We don't want a war."

"Oh, you won't get one, but..."

"Her father doesn't know that," Yvette finished for him.

"Right."

Yvette turned to Emiko who was still sitting on the couch looking lost and entirely too pale. She walked toward the girl and held out her hand, "Come on chéri, let's get you packed for a few days."

"Yoroshii."

"Emiko," The girl looked up at Yvette's questioning tone, "I don't speak Japanese."

A pink blush flooded Emiko's face; she went from sheet white to beet red as she realized that she had answered in the wrong language. "I am sorry. I..."

"Emiko, it's okay, I just don't know what you said."

"She said, 'Very well'."

Yvette turned to Xavier "How…"

"Some friends were good at linguis--"Xavier trailed off as the pain slammed him. Shawn and Lance had been super geeks when it came to learning a new language. He had been lucky if he could remember "hello" in each one they learned. He could say the greeting in twelve languages, but other than a smattering of other words, that was it for him.

Yvette could see the pain in Xavier's face, a physical pain caused by a memory. She could hear his breathing become rapid and heavy. She watched as he gripped the desk turning his knuckles white. His whole body began to shake, and his eyes glazed over.

"Emiko, call that number. I think he needs his friend."

Emiko took the slip of paper and dialed.

"Rogers," was the answer.

"Is this Xavier's friend?"

Sam went dead still. "Yes."

"He is at my apartment and he seems…"

"Is he hurt?" Sam asked quickly.

"No."

"Are you hurt?"

"No."

"Is anyone hurt?"

"No, please, he seems very scared."

"What's your address?"

Emiko told Sam the address and added, "Please hurry. Yvette is here, she is trying to talk to him, please."

"Oh God, tell her to not touch him. He could hurt her very badly, very quickly."

"Hai," and the line went dead.

"Yvette, the man said not to touch him. He said he could hurt you."

Yvette knew what could happen when you touched someone in a stress-induced trance like this. She couldn't see what he was reliving like she had a few times with other people, but she could feel the pain he was in. *'Damn, how does Cassandra do this all day?'* Yvette was winded and in pain after only a few seconds of Xavier being trapped. Yvette stood back out of arm's reach and a little to the side; she began singing the lullaby her mother had used on her and her siblings for years. No matter what the nightmare, it soothed them all.

She could see Emiko standing near the couch, the phone still clutched in her hand, shaking. Yvette really couldn't muster the energy to calm both of them at the same time. She would pick up the pieces of Emiko and bring them to Anne; she would fix all of it.

When Yvette felt the wind through the now open door, she stepped back quickly as Xavier felt it. He lunged for the one standing in the door.

CHAPTER THIRTEEN

"SAVER STOP!" Sam side stepped the Marine and knocked him to the ground. "XAVIER, COME OUT OF IT! DAMN IT! XAVIER, YOU'RE SAFE, XAVIER IT'S OVER, YOU'RE HOME! YOU'RE HERE!" Sam struggled to get the frightened Marine under control, when a second set of hands helped to pin him. He looked at the woman next to him. "You need to get back, ma'am, he would never be able to live with himself if he hurt you when he was like this."

"Sir, I have two brothers and a sister; none of them has ever taken me, and one of them is a gold medal winning wrestler."

"Bit different from Xavier, here."

"He won't hurt me," she said with confidence.

Emiko couldn't stand it anymore. Xavier was in so much pain from whatever memory had trapped him. She knelt down and crawled over to the pile of limbs, finding the one covered in camouflage; she began rubbing the hand attached.

"Xavier," she said softly, "you need to be calm. You need to find a safe place in your heart."

The struggling slowed but did not stop. "Xavier, I do not know where you are or what you are seeing, but there are friends here who want to help you, who want to see you," Tears rolled down the cheeks of both Emiko and Xavier.

Never breaking contact with the Marine, Emiko moved so she was leaning over his head. She began stroking his hair as Yvette had done to her earlier when she had her own breakdown.

"Xavier, we need you to come back. Xavier, are you here? Are you back with us?" The man stopped struggling, Yvette and Sam moved off him but still near enough that they could quickly restrain him if the need arose.

When the weight left Xavier's body he rolled to his side, shaking, then curled in on himself, still caught in his personal living hell. "No, no, I can't, no, no, no, no, nonononononononono no."

Emiko kept stroking his hair. Sam stood up and called Max; this was above all of them. Xavier might need something more than a soothing voice. Sam hoped his friend wasn't gone all together. "I should have made Max go see him months ago. God, I should have done something."

"Max, good, get over to 689 Oak, now. Xavier's having a flashback, and we can't get him out of it. He's curled up into a little ball saying 'no' repeatedly. I don't know what set it off or how the two girls knew to call me, but man, he needs you."

"Shit, I just drove past there. I'll be there in two."

"Third floor, man, door's open."

True to his word, Max slid in the open door two minutes later. A very long two minutes as Xavier was still the same.

"Nononononononnononononononon onononono"

"Xavier," Max said, kneeling next to Emiko, "Xavier, I know it hurts, son. I know it's the worst feeling ever, to keep seeing them that way."

Emiko started to pull away, but Max shook his head and then tipped it toward her hand where it rested on Xavier's head. When she started stroking again, he nodded. She shifted her posture a little making it easier to use both hands

111 | P a g e

on his hair so that she was always touching him.

Max smiled widely and nodded again, still talking to Xavier. "I wasn't there, Xavier, but I know what happened. You know there was nothing you could do, you know that," Xavier uncurled some but was still on his side shaking. Max was thinking he might have to sedate him but he was afraid it wouldn't help, and Xavier would just be trapped in his nightmare, unable to surface when his mind was ready to move past this episode.

Emiko was on her knees and when Xavier uncurled, he put his head in her lap. She slid her legs so they were to the side of her and kept stroking Xavier.

Max paused, lost in thought and Xavier noted the silence. He moved to curl in on himself again, but before he could, Emiko began to sing to him.

> "nen nen ocororiyo, ocororiyo
> boya wa yoiko da, nen ne shina
> boya no omori wa, doko e itta
> ano yama koete, sato e itta
> sato no miyage ni nani morota
> den den daiko ni, sho no fue"

As Emiko sang the little song, Xavier rolled onto his back, blinking as if the sun hurt him, he moved to cover his eyes but the room went dark before he could. Yvette had pulled the curtains, then grabbed the throw off the back of the couch, and draped it over the trio on the floor.

Sam raised an eyebrow at her actions.

"Not the only wounded vet in the world," she replied to the unasked question.

Sam nodded in understanding; she apparently knew better than he what Xavier needed. He had never watched someone have a flashback. He followed her with his eyes when she went into the kitchen, found a cup, filled it with tea, warmed it, and rummaged around in more cupboards until she found some crackers. He couldn't believe it when she opened the plastic making no noise at all. No one could open those things without waking the dead.

Sam's attention went back to his friend when Xavier's boots moved as he tried to pull his legs up under the blanket, and he heard Xavier say in a shaky voice that he was cold. Sam turned toward the nearest bedroom, pulled the comforter off the bed, and added it to the throw already on Xavier. He was grateful when the tall Marine once again straightened out his body. Seeing someone as tall as Xavier curled up that small made Sam's joints ache in sympathy.

Yvette was done in the kitchen. She tapped Max on the shoulder and he slid his head out of the makeshift blanket fort that he and Emiko shared with Xavier. In her hands were the tea and the crackers.

"There is a little bit of sugar in there to help with the aftershocks."

Max nodded again, taking the offered snack and ducked back under the blanket.

Yvette walked to where Sam was standing, tipping her head toward the kitchen. "Come on," she whispered.

Curious, he followed. She opened the refrigerator as Sam leaned against the counter. "So who's got the PTSD in your family?" he asked.

"Mmm, a better question would be: who doesn't?"

"That bad?"

"No, most days it's fine."

"So what happened today?" Sam jerked his head to the living room.

"I'm not sure," If the tone in her voice was any indication, not knowing was not something she encountered often and that, when it did, it seriously pissed her off. "I came to see how Emiko was doing. Her parents called the shop to talk to her about the mugging."

"Ah, wait, the shop?"

"Don't ask. Her parents are screwed up."

"Okay."

"She and I were talking about how she didn't have to go back to Japan, even if her father did show up to take her back. Xavier said that he could get his useless undeserving ass back on the plane. That was the first time I'd seen him. Emiko recognized him fast enough."

"From what I understand, they had lunch earlier. Okay, after her parents called, I'm guessing, they split and he ended up with me and she ended up here."

115 | P a g e

"Yeah, it's been about five hours since they called, I couldn't get away as fast as I wanted. Then it took me about a half hour to get her to answer the door."

"Hmmm."

"What set off the..." Sam shrugged his shoulders, not really knowing what to call Xavier's episode.

"Emiko said something in Japanese that he understood. Um, she said, 'Very well.' And when I asked how he knew what it meant, he started to say that he knew people who were good with languages. Then he was just gone. When you opened the door the breeze startled him enough to make him attack, I guess."

"Crap," Sam made a move to punch the counter, but Yvette caught his hand.

"That will not help you or him."

"I should have known better. I knew he's been skittish, and more so the last two days. Damn it, that's the second time today that he's rounded on me," Sam walked over to the entryway to the kitchen where he could see the group still under the blanket. "What's with the dark, anyway?"

"Oh, my brother always has migraines after an attack, and the light hurts."

"Oh, okay."

"And the tea and crackers are so if he throws up, then it's something more than Jim Beam."

"Fuck."

It was Yvette's turn to raise an eyebrow, "What?"

"When I found him, apparently just after he sent Emiko home, I took him to meet Max," Sam said, tipping his head toward the living room, "and then we went to 8th Street Ale House and had a couple pints. Fuck. Fuck. Fuck. His commander was there when we came out, just bad timing. I guess he happened to be in the neighborhood, but Saver was already worked up, and the colonel made it worse."

Yvette waited to see if he would explain how the colonel made it worse, but he didn't; he just continued on, "Saver hailed a cab and went home, but if he was drinking JB, then..."

Yvette finished for him, "He went home to get drunk, to forget."

"Yeah. I'm guessing that didn't work, if he was here for this to go down. However, if it was going to happen, at least it was around someone, instead of alone in his apartment."

***

Emiko continued to stroke Xavier's hair the entire time the man talked to him. She had picked up that his name was Max and assumed that he was some sort of psychiatrist. It was getting stuffy under the blankets, but Emiko put together that the light was hurting Xavier's eyes when Max had gotten the snack from Yvette, and Xavier flinched.

Hoping to help, Emiko offered, "Maybe we should go into my room. I have very dark curtains and shades as well; the bed would be nicer on your back than this hard floor. If you are still cold, I can get more blankets. Then you would be able to sit up and drink the tea and try to eat something, if that is a good thing for you to do," She looked at Max for confirmation that these things were wise.

Xavier bolted up. "Oh God, I'm sorry, your legs, oh hell," he turned toward the desk grabbing the trash basket before emptying what little was in his stomach into the bin.

Max dashed to the kitchen and smiled at Yvette as she handed him a bottle of water, "Thanks," and he was gone again. "Come on Marine, get it out."

"Oh God, there's..." Xavier dry heaved, "nothing..." once more dry heaving, "left."

"When was the last time you ate?"

"He ate at lunch but I think that is already..."

Xavier rasped, "Oh yeah, gone..."

"Hmm, I can see that," Max said as Xavier moved away from the basket. With a quickness that came from experience, Max had the bucket dumped, rinsed and returned before Xavier needed it again.

"Not your first go with this kinda thing, doc?" Xavier whispered his throat raw from both the bile and the emotions he had just churned up.

"Not my first dance with the porcelain gods, no."

"Oh God, doc, don't make me laugh; everything hurts."

"Pain reminds us we're alive."

Xavier's eyes glassed over for a second until Emiko started petting his hair again and singing the lullaby she had been singing before.

"What is that?" Xavier asked.

"Nene Cororiyo," she replied after finishing the little song.

"What is it?" he asked again.

"It is a Japanese lullaby, though we do not really have lullabies."

"What does it mean in English," Xavier asked, sounding more like a small boy than a big Marine. Emiko sang it again in English this time.

"Go to sleep, go to sleep

you are a good boy, go to sleep

where did your nanny go

she crossed over a mountain and went to her village

what souvenir did you get from her village

a small drum and a flute."

Max sat back and watched the pair; Emiko was the key to bringing Xavier back. In Max's career, he had learned that when a vet loses himself as deeply as Xavier had, someone is needed to guide him back. Sometimes this person is a partner in crime so to speak; one of the wounded vet's friends, a guy from the unit, his brother of choice. Sometimes it is a parent or close family member, but more often, it is the spouse, the wife waiting for him. If there are none of these people, then in his experience the vet never comes back. He will always be lost in whatever situation has broken his mind to start with. There might be times where they surface, but the incident will always haunt them and forever be in the back of their minds growing, until it takes them over.

"You wanna try standing up slowly this time?" Max asked.

"Yeah, don't want to lie down though, head's not too bad."

"Alright, I think Yvette threw some light food together. You should get some of it into you; you need more than crackers."

When Xavier tried to stand, his legs gave out from underneath him. Sam and Max caught him before he fell, completely crushing poor Emiko under him. She had been standing in front of him.

"Fuck, hate this God damn shit," Xavier said as Max and Sam got him situated so they could more easily bear his full weight. "Weak as a newborn fawn, what ass comes up with this shit?"

"Saver it's alright. Let us take care of you."

"Sam."

"Shush man, we got it."

"Not the point," Xavier complained as they all but poured him into the kitchen chair.

Yvette set a plate of cheeses, meats, and light toast in front of him. "Try the toast first," She offered.

Xavier looked up at her not knowing what to say, "Um, sorry about..."

"Don't. It's all right. We all have our fantômes to deal with."

"Still, it wasn't yours."

"Xavier, chéri, it is my cross to bear because you are tied to Emiko in some way, and I am hers for as long as she will keep me," Yvette told the Marine, her accent getting thicker with every word.

Xavier thought maybe he was losing it 'cause for a second he swore she was a lot bigger, taller, more...well just more. Her coloring darkened, too, her eyes going so dark blue they looked almost black and her hair turning a deeper shade of red. He felt like Bilbo when Gandalf made him leave "the one ring". Not sure, he saw what he saw but knowing damn good and well he saw what he saw.

Yvette chuckled as she watched Xavier shake his head and reach for the toast. "Good chéri, good."

Xavier ate slowly, making sure each bite stayed down before taking another. Yvette left him to join the others in the living room.

"Max, is he ok?" Sam asked.

"For the moment."

"Look Max, you talk to his CO yet?" Sam hoped.

"No, that was the plan for this afternoon. I don't want him alone, though. I'm sure he won't have another attack, but I'm also sure if left to his own devices, he will do what he has been doing."

"Drinking and sleeping," Sam supplied.

"Yeah."

"I've got too many people at my place. I'll crash at…" the cop started to say.

But Emiko spoke up, "I would like to stay with him."

Max looked at the girl.

Yvette looked at her as well. She started to object to the idea, but Emiko started first.

"My father would never know I was there. He may be able to find your addresses and come looking for me at your house or Melissa's or even Anne's house. He would not think of looking for me at Xavier's. If he did, we all know Xavier would be able to scare him away just by speaking."

"Emiko, what if something happens and Xavier goes under again?" Sam asked.

"I will call Max."

"Emiko I live outside of town, it would take too much time for me to get there."

"I won't hurt her," Xavier said from the doorway.

"Xavier you've swung at me twice in one day."

"I won't hurt her," he said again. "I'll sleep on the couch, she can take the bed. You'll pick me up at ten, she can come with or we can drop her off at one of the girls' houses; Melissa sounds best in case Mr. Nara pops up."

Everyone turned to Max; Sam was the first to speak, "Well, Max?"

Max knew there was no way to know Xavier wouldn't have another break, but he needed to start building a rapport with the Marine. Xavier needed to know Max trusted him. As late as it was getting, they would just sleep and part ways. He knew, though, that Xavier would have nightmares. "Xavier, let me give you a sedative so you sleep. Something to…"

"They don't work," he said before Max could finish, "I have tried them all."

"What about…"

Xavier interrupted again, "Even the new one that came out last month."

Max thought for another minute. "If you're both sure?"

"Yes," two voices answered.

"Xavier, where is your place?" Yvette asked.

He turned to her, "Sixth and Market."

"Emiko, if anything happens, go to Melissa's and call Max."

Feeling like a broken record, Xavier repeated, "I will not hurt her."

"Not awake, no, but if you get…" Yvette answered, having seen what her brother could do when caught in a night terror.

"Damn it, if I have to, I will stay awake."

"You need your rest, Xavier," Max insisted.

"Oh for Christ's sake, I didn't hurt anyone today," Xavier's voice rose with his anger.

"You could have," Sam again was the gloomy Gus. Of course, he had been at the end of Xavier's fist, too.

"Make up your minds; either I'm safe for society or I'm not," With that said, he turned, "bring her or don't, I don't care," And then he left.

"Fuck!" Sam shouted.

"Sam," Yvette admonished him.

"Sorry."

Yvette shook her head again while Max did the same thing. "That did not go how I would have liked. Emiko, do you think you can handle it if he goes under again?" Max asked.

"Hai, yes," Emiko said, correcting herself. "I will try not to use Japanese while there; it seemed to be the..." she hesitated, searching for the right word, "trigger." She spoke unsurely until Max nodded. "It seemed to be the trigger," She felt terrible for causing Xavier to relive whatever horrible memory it was.

Max looked confused, "Wait, why would..."

"The boys," Sam paused, "did you get his file?"

"Yeah I read about his friends."

"Ok, they had a knack for languages; last I heard was 16. Xavier never was that good, but he understood a bit."

"He knew she said 'very well'," Yvette added. "I asked him how he knew; he started to answer and then flipped out. I've seen the look on my brother, so I knew what was happening. Talking with him usually helps, so after I told Emiko to call

Sam, I tried talking to him. It wasn't until Sam opened the door that there was a problem."

"How much noise did you make?" Max asked trying to get a full picture of what triggered Xavier's flashback.

"I didn't."

"He did not."

"He didn't," The three answered at the same time.

"The breeze from the hallway startled him. Sam could not have known," Emiko explained.

"Okay, Emiko, I think it will be okay for you to stay with Xavier, if it is what you want to do."

"Yes, I do."

"Get some stuff then."

Max asked as she left, "Why isn't she staying here? What is the problem?"

"Xavier stopped a mugging with Emiko as the victim. Her parents found out and called saying they were taking her back to Japan. She doesn't want to go."

Max knew Emiko couldn't go; he would need her. "I take it her parents are overbearing?"

"That's putting it mildly, more like controlling," Yvette complained.

"Hmmm."

Emiko came out of her room with a small bag but ducked into the bathroom a moment later. She reappeared placing a few more items in her bag. "I am ready."

"Sam, you..." Max started.

"Yep, come on Emiko."

Sam paused at the desk to jot something down on a scrap of paper. "Here is Xavier's number and address," he said, giving the paper to Yvette. "Mine's on the back."

CHAPTER FOURTEEN

Xavier slammed his apartment door. Even at his absolute worst, back in the beginning, he had never hurt anyone. "Damn it!" he stormed into the kitchen barely conscious of making a sandwich. At least he'd found his Jeep. He had taken a second taxi over to MY SWEET DREAMS, then decided to check on Emiko, remembering her reaction to the phone call. Turns out both Mr. and Mrs. Nara were being asses. Out of habit, he reached for the Jim Beam but pulled up short. "Fuck," He opened the fridge: no milk, no juice, and no pop. Knowing better than to drink the water out of the kitchen faucet, he wandered to the bathroom. He considered taking a shower. He was still ice cold from his flashback, but he didn't want to be in the shower if they deemed him safe to watch over Emiko.

Xavier meandered back to the living room. He had lived in this apartment for three years...scratch that, he had existed here for three years; he knew he had stopped living the day Lance and Shawn died.

They may not have been his brothers or lovers, but damn it, he loved them. He would have gladly exchanged his life for both of their lives because, as individuals or as a couple, Xavier felt they were far more worthy of life than he was.

He sat down on the couch that had come with the apartment. In truth, Xavier owned nothing but his clothes. He wasn't even sure if the sheets were his.

Xavier jumped at the knock on the door. Cursing under his breath, he opened it and found Sam and Emiko there. "So I'm good enough?" Xavier sneered as he flung the door open.

"Damn it, Saver, knock it off," Sam pushed Xavier's shoulder. "We were thinking of you. What if you had had that flashback and Yvette and I weren't there? I couldn't keep you down by myself."

"Sam, in three years, I have never hurt anyone. Did I hurt you? No! I took a swing, yes, but I never made contact. Fuck, Sam," Xavier spun on his heel toward the kitchen and stopped. "Stay with her, I'm going to the store," Slamming the door behind him, he stood in the hall, took a deep breath, and trotted down the stairs. He debated whether to drive or to walk; he decided it was better to drive so he could get more while at the store.

Once there Xavier went through the store grabbing chips, snacks and drinks. The girl at the checkout stand looked at him strangely. He shrugged his shoulders, paid for his groceries, and made it back home, having only been gone fifteen minutes.

***

"Damn, that boy is starting to get on my last nerve."

"What was he like before?" Emiko questioned quietly.

Sam looked at her while he decided what would be the best answer. "He was outgoing; he was happy, always smiling, joking, and making other people smile by just being there. He never shied away from hard work. He, Shawn, Lance, and Lisa were the four musketeers. They were always together, since they were this high," Sam lowered his hand to knee level.

132 | P a g e

"Trouble makers?" Emiko asked hoping she got the right term again.

"No, they were good kids. Lisa, well, she tried to stir up trouble, but they kept her grounded...uh, level headed, made her behave. She grew up into a fine young lady because of those three."

"What happened to them, to him?" She said it so softly Sam didn't hear her but Xavier did from the door.

"We died," was Xavier's answer, "but my body didn't get the message. There are snacks and drinks. I didn't know what you went for, so I grabbed some of a lot of different things. I'm hitting the shower, then the bed, or in this case, the couch."

When the water could be heard hitting the tile, Emiko looked at Sam, "Please tell me."

"I don't know all of it, just a bit. They were in Afghanistan, and they were captured. The leader had killed Lance, then Shawn, and had turned to kill Xavier when the opposition, guess you could call them, attacked the compound where they were being held," Sam supplied with a shrug. He continued, "They didn't finish Xavier, left him to die in the rubble, but the good guys found him, *found them*, brought them back. He was patched up and we were given their bodies to bury. The problem is, like Saver said, he died that day, too, just not physically."

"Why do you call him that, 'Saver'?"

"Hmm," Sam smiled for the first time since he saw Saver in Magical Ways, "When they were still in high school, he wanted to be a EMT. Took the classes and did all the training on his own time, the youngest ever in our county to be certified," Emiko nodded, she could see that in him.

"He was called to a fire, well, an explosion followed by a fire. Do you know what a meth lab is?"

Emiko had only a vague idea, so she shrugged her shoulders, "Maybe."

"Meth is a drug, but it is very unstable and very dangerous to make it. Takes a lot of unstable chemicals, and if they're not kept just right, they explode and most cooks use their own product so they are not very safe."

She nodded understanding.

"The fire was going; one of our firefighters went into this crappy little trailer to ensure there wasn't anyone trapped in the damn thing. Jerry ended up getting his coat or something caught on a beam that had fallen. Xavier saw him struggling through one of the windows, so being the brave dumbass he is, he ran in there, not even thinking of the danger to himself, and got Jerry out."

Clutching his robe shut tightly, Xavier said, "Fire Chief called me the Saver's Saver, and the name stuck."

Neither one had noticed the water shut off, or the man under discussion walk into the room. Turning back around, he went into his bedroom.

Watching the door this time, Emiko asked, "Do you think he will be how he was before?"

Sam stood, stretched, and answered her the best he could. "No, I think he is forever changed, but I think enough of him is still there that someone closer to who he was before can be found. He just has to decide to look for that man. I think he needs a reason to find him, and for three years he hasn't had one."

Both fell into silence when Xavier came out of his room. "What," he asked them, "waiting for me to freak again?"

"Just noticing what a fine looking man you've grown into."

"Oh, for Christ's sake Sam, I was grown when I left."

"No, you were an adult, but you weren't grown yet."

"So what, I don't look the same?"

"No, you do, you just seem less, I don't know. You always had...hell, this is girl talk, I don't know what I mean, you just look different, that's all," Sam almost mentioned that Shawn and Lance would look different, too, but thought better about it before he did. Xavier didn't need another flashback tonight. Max would be hard enough on him tomorrow.

Seeing the clock, Xavier asked Emiko, "Do you want to go to sleep or...?" he left the question unfinished.

Sam's phone went off. "Well shit, it's dispatch. Rogers. Yeah sure, got it."

"Problem?" Xavier asked when he hung up.

"No, maybe. Robbery near Crystal's shop. They know I'm friends with Max and

Crystal so they gave me a call as a heads up. I'll head over and see what's going on. Hope it's not those asses again. Crystal's been through enough as it is."

After Sam left, Xavier broke the silence and asked, "Did you want something to drink?"

"Um, do you have any tea?" Emiko answered.

Xavier pawed around in the bags trying to remember if he'd bought any, and finding that he hadn't, he shook his head. "Sorry. I have milk and cran-raspberry juice."

"The juice please."

Getting a glass and some ice he poured her a glass and then got one for himself, too.

"Thank you."

"No problem."

She took the glass, walked to his small window and looked out.

"Not much of a view, I'm sorry to say," he commented.

"It is nice just the same; do children play in the playground?"

"I, uh, I don't know."

"Do you not look out?"

"No, I..." He knew if he told her he tried to sleep twenty-four hours a day that he would sound pathetic, so he just didn't finish.

"Are you sad you did not die with your friends?"

Xavier coughed on the juice; no one had asked so directly before.

Emiko knew she should not have asked the question as soon as she spoke. "I am sorry, I should not."

"No, it's, it's fine. I, hmmm, I think Max should be around for that answer, 'cause some days it's yes and some days, no I'm not sad, I'm angry."

Xavier looked so lost, so worn that Emiko's heart cried for him. She ached to comfort him, to make him feel...well, she just didn't know what she felt. She sat next to him on the couch, "I am glad you are here. I will always be glad that you lived that day. I am sorry that your friends died and that you miss them. Am I a bad person for being glad that your places were not changed? Because I think that they would not have been there yesterday to stop that man or that they would not have let me into their home to hide from my parents. I do not think I would have been..." Emiko stopped. She was about to say she would not have been as confused by them either, but the look on Xavier's face gave her pause.

"Emiko, do you, hmmm...never mind," Xavier changed his mind mid-thought.

"Do I what?" Her voice was small; her stomach felt weird again, she was sure it was her body reacting to Xavier. She had finally figured out it was telling her that she liked him and that she wanted to feel his lips on hers again.

"Can I kiss you?" He whispered in a voice as small as hers had been.

Her throat went dry and she knew she would never be able to get the words out. In the end, she just nodded.

He leaned in very slowly and as he leaned, she leaned back until the arm of the couch stopped her, then their lips met. The instant they did, Emiko sighed, and Xavier groaned.

Emiko was trying to forget the tight feeling in her stomach. She gasped when his hand glided over her side, his thumb brushing her breast, every stroke made her tighten to the point of pain. "Xavier," she whimpered.

"God, Emiko, I don't think I can keep away from you."

"I do not know what I feel, my stomach is tight, and I cannot breathe."

Xavier bit his tongue to keep from laughing. "Emiko, it's because you're aroused, you want me to keep doing what I'm doing, or at least your body does. You seriously have never been with anyone?"

"No," she whispered, "you are the first person to kiss me, to touch me in any way," She ducked her head embarrassed by her lack of experience.

"Ah Emiko, honey, it's ok."

"I should know how..." the girl started to say.

"No, you shouldn't know sweetie, really, you're not knowing is a..." Xavier paused trying to decide how to tell her that her innocence was a turn on, but that she would still be wanted after she learned. "A little crash course in men and attraction. To most men being innocent and a virgin are good things. Men like that they get to teach the woman how things feel. It's an honor. A, uh, a cherished experience. And later we like it when you do know what to do because we know that it's because of us. It's an ego thing."

Emiko nodded her head once, understanding most of what he was saying. Emiko did know the basics of a man and woman being together and she wanted to know more, she just hoped she would be good enough to make Xavier happy. She wanted to keep him smiling like he had earlier and like he was now. The smile now was a soft smile, making his eyes gentle, making them shimmer with an inner light. Emiko was hoping the smile was because of her but her own inner doubts told her it was just because he was going to get to have sex, her self-confidence nonexistent as it was.

Timidly Emiko reached out and touched his cheek with the back of her hand. He leaned his face into her touch. She turned her hand so that now she was cupping his cheek with her palm. He closed his eyes, memorizing the feeling of her delicate hand against his face. He knew that there should never be anything between them and that he was not really the man who could give her everything she needed. But sometimes knowing a thing and doing a thing are different.

He leaned back down tasting her lips. Xavier rubbed his nose to hers, and she giggled. "Thought I would show you another kind of kiss."

She looked at him with confusion.

"An Eskimo kiss," and he did it again.

"Why would people kiss like that?"

"Because it's too cold to kiss with lips, they might freeze off, so just noses," he said, hoping she would giggle again - it was a beautiful sound.

"I thought those were for children."

"Oh no, no they're not just for children." He kissed a line to her neck. Then he alternated between kissing and Eskimo kissing his way down her neck until he found the spot right in the crook of her neck that made her moan and arch up into his body. "Oh darling you are so wonderful."

Beep beep beep beep beep.

Xavier and Emiko both jumped at the loud noise coming from under his window.

Beep beep beep.

He dropped his head so that it rested on Emiko's forehead and said, "That would be the alarm on my Jeep."

"Maybe you should go turn it off before your neighbors become angry."

"Yeah, yeah, don't move."

Xavier drug himself away from the couch grabbing his keys from the table, opened the window and tried to silence the alarm. That didn't work so he said, "I'll be right back," stepping to the door.

Emiko snuggled into the couch. She felt warm and fuzzy, happy and content. She closed her eyes enjoying how she felt.

***

Xavier bounded up the steps two at a time. When he made it back to his apartment, he found Emiko asleep on his couch. Smiling he watched her for a moment and then gently he slid his arms under her neck and knees and carried her to his bed. Careful not to wake her, he laid her down. Her hair fanned out around her like a raven-colored angel's crown.

A chill ran down his spine making him shiver. With care, he tenderly gathered her hair, sliding it to one side.

Murmuring something in Japanese, Emiko rolled to her side, sliding her little hands under his pillow. His heart seized as several emotions hit. The longing and lust were hard to ignore, but they were beat out by his mind as it brought forward memories of long hours listening to Lance talk about his love for and obsession with all things Oriental. They had laughed once because he said if he ever went straight, it would only be for an Asian girl. It had been part of what started Lance and Shawn's relationship, and it had always been an inside joke between the two. Shawn would pick out a girl and say, "Is she the one to steal you from me?" Lance would answer, "Nope, too short."

Emiko spoke again in Japanese pulling Xavier from his thoughts; he was glad that it hadn't manifested into a full flashback.

He noticed she was shivering. He pulled his comforter over her, but the shivering only lessened. He shrugged, looked up at the ceiling and said, "You had better leave me alone tonight you bastards or we will have a problem," Trying not to disturb Emiko, he climbed under the blanket curling around the small girl.

Within a minute two things happened: Xavier fell into a dreamless sleep and Emiko stopped shivering. Neither one moved for some time after tangling themselves into a pile of arms and legs. Somewhere around dawn, Emiko pulled herself free, wandering sleepily to the bathroom. After answering Mother Nature's call, she more or less sleepwalked back to Xavier, re-tangled herself with him, and continued to sleep peacefully.

CHAPTER FIFTEEN

The insistent pounding in his head woke Xavier. He found that it wasn't *in* his head but on his door. An odd pressure on his right side started to panic him.

When he tried moving, Emiko spoke in her sleep. "No. No.

go to sleep, go to sleep
you are a good boy, go to sleep
where did your nanny go
she crossed over a mountain and went to her village

what souvenir did you get from her village

a small drum and a flute."

Xavier patted Emiko's cheek lightly. "Honey, Emiko, I need my right side back. Emiko," Xavier said a little louder to make it heard over the knocking at the door. He shook his head. "The little angel sleeps like the dead."

He heard Sam yell his name, the cop's voice verging on panic. Xavier didn't want to startle Emiko but he needed to let Sam know they were ok.

Cringing he yelled, "SAM, BE THERE IN A SECOND!"

"XAVIER, WHERE'S THE DAMN SPARE?!"

"Spare what?" he mumbled to himself. "Like I'm going to have a key lying around to my safe place," he said, still grumbling.

Xavier pulled himself free from the pretty zombie and stumbled to the door. "Damn it, the wench put half my body to sleep."

"What wench?" Sam asked as the door opened.

"Emiko," he answered off handedly.

"What, you slept with Emiko? You bastard, she had a hell of a -"

"Oh quit, Sam. Yes, we slept, heavy on the sleep part. She fell asleep on the couch I put her in my bed and she couldn't stop shivering, so I climbed in to warm her up. That's all."

"Oh," Sam answered with chagrin.

"Yeah, 'oh.' What time is it?" the bleary man asked.

"10:15"

"Crap."

"Yeah, I've been out here for 20 minutes; I'm sure your neighbors hate you right now."

"Well shit, let me see if I can get dead girl to wake up."

"Huh?"

"Apparently, Emiko sleeps like the dead. She didn't wake up to me yelling in her ear at you."

"Why would you yell in her ear?"

"Because we were all tangled up. I was trying to get untangled, and you were starting to panic."

"Was not."

Xavier retorted back, "Were too."

"Whatever. She didn't wake up?"

"Nope, not even after me yelling or pulling free."

Sam shook his head. "That's a heavy sleeper."

"Yeah, though when I told her I needed my right side back she said no and started singing that lullaby again."

"The nanny one?" Sam said questioningly.

"Yeah," Xavier stopped at his door. She was in the middle of his bed looking lost and confused, knees pulled to her chest rocking back and forth. "Emiko," he said softly, knowing all too well that loud sounds could scare the crap out of someone like this.

"Xavier," she whispered back, "he took you."

"Who?"

"Otosan."

Xavier grappled with his limited language skills to find the word he was looking for; his skills were always hit or miss.

"Emiko, I don't know..." Xavier started, lowering himself onto the bed, trying hard not to move it.

"She said 'my father'," Sam said. "It's one of the few I know."

"Otosan came and pulled you from me. I was not strong enough to keep you here."

Xavier's lips twitched in a ghost of a smile. "Silly girl, you are so strong, you just can't see it."

She shook her head coming out of her nightmare a little more, "No, no, you are strong."

"Emiko, yes I am physically strong, but I am not as strong as you."

She just kept shaking her head. "No, no, no."

Xavier placed a hand on either side of her face, keeping her from shaking it, and said, "Little Emiko is so brave, she tells a man with a knife to her throat, 'no.' She tells a big psycho Marine, 'no.' She tells a shrink that she will stay by herself with the big psycho Marine for a night."

"I am not strong," she whispered.

"Yes, you are," he whispered into her ear and hugged her tightly. "You are the strongest person I've ever known. Now, Sam is here, and I have to get ready to go to Max's barbeque. Do you want to go with us?"

One nod of her head was all he got as an answer. "Ok. Do you want to take a shower?"

"You can use it first."

"I don't really need to. I'll get dressed while you shower."

"Alright," She slipped off his bed and past Sam quietly.

"I always wondered how those ninja myths got started, you know about them being so quiet and all."

Sam chuckled. "Yeah, because they never taught you to walk softly and carry a big stick, man."

"But she doesn't even stir the air."

"Xavier, have you seen her? She's a walking piece of paper. She's so light and... well, you are not a piece of paper."

"Yeah, yeah, anyway, out, so I can change."

"Fine," Sam left the Marine to change alone.

When he pulled his shirt off, he caught site of himself in the mirror over the dresser. Pale, thin scars covered his chest where his captors had sliced him open with razor blades. His shoulder was a mass of corded scars left by the shrapnel and debris from the RPG that had taken out the bunker where they held him. Below those and a little to the right was a single round scar from the bullet that had been meant to kill him. His back was nearly as bad. So cliché, but someone had liked whips, and so there were dozens of whip marks on his back. He knew if he shaved his hair to Marine Corps regs there would be patches that would show where he had no hair - more shrapnel and debris, none of it life threatening, but it still damned the skin and so no hair grew.

He wondered for a minute if the colonel would make him get a regulation haircut if he took him up on the mission. Xavier really didn't want everyone to see those scars. His chest and back would stay covered, but head covers had to be removed inside, no way to hide them.

"Xavier, where did Emiko put her bag, she can't find it," Sam walked in on the shirtless man.

"Fuck," they said simultaneously.

"Get out!" Xavier demanded.

"Sorry Saver."

"Sam, stop that."

"What, you said to get out, I was leaving," Sam said with his back to Xavier giving the man some privacy.

"No, stop calling me Saver," Xavier said quietly. "He died that day."

"No, just hid to keep you safe, like Saver's supposed to."

"He's not a separate person; it's me."

"Yep, I know. Talk to Max about it. I'm pretty sure I know what he's gonna say without all the mumbo jumbo big words."

Wanting to stop the conversation from going any farther, Xavier answered Sam's first question. "Emiko's bag is behind the couch."

"Fine," Understanding that the discussion was closed for now, Sam left.

***

Emiko found the bag where Sam said it would be and rushed into Xavier's bathroom.

She turned on the shower and quickly adjusted the temperature. She wanted to be ready as soon as she could. She had a bad feeling that her father was coming and she could not shake it. She hoped that if she were far away he would give up and go home. Emiko knew that she would inherit something when her parents passed, but if it meant them leaving her alone in her new life in America, she would happily disinherit herself.

Lost in her thoughts she washed her hair and body through routine. She shaved her legs and arms the same way until her inattention caused her to cut her leg with the razor, crying out in surprise.

She dropped the razor and just stood there, looking at the blood trickle down her leg.

Sam heard Emiko shout as he walked by on his way to the kitchen. Tapping on the door, he asked, "Are you ok?"

Snapping out of her fugue state, Emiko answered, "Hai, I cut my leg, I will be fine."

"When you get out, use some toilet paper on the cut. It will stop the bleeding."

Emiko raised an eyebrow at the thought but was willing to try it. "Hai," she replied.

Rinsing the conditioner out of her hair, she turned off the water, wrung the water out of her long hair and reached for a towel. Drying off, she wondered what she should wear; she really had just randomly grabbed what was on top in her dresser drawers. Poking through her bag, she found panties and a matching bra. She had never worn this set before. They were pale jade lace with darker jade straps and a matching bow on the panties. They were very low cut. Not her usual style, but she had bought them with the intention of wearing them on her honeymoon. Another reach into the bag found a slim light green skirt and a white silk tank top. Nothing else in the bag was suitable for a party of any kind.

Brushing her hair out, after putting her clothes on, she tried to decide if she should leave it loose or braid it. Looking in her bag once more, she found she had not brought any ties, so she left it loose.

Melissa had shown her how to apply makeup to play up her eyes. She carefully followed every step Melissa had told her. When she finished she nodded at the image in the mirror, cleaned up the bathroom, and opened the door to find both men sitting in the living room in silence.

155 | P a g e

CHAPTER SIXTEEN

She looked at Xavier's sad, lost face and Sam's angry, determined face and knew something had happened while she was in her shower to hurt their renewed friendship.

"I am ready," she said softly so as to not frighten Xavier.

Sam stood and looked at her. He stared for a moment and kicked Xavier's boot. Xavier's head snapped up and he looked as if he was about to yell at Sam, but Sam tipped his head in Emiko's direction. Xavier turned and his mouth fell open.

"Uh, um, uh..." Xavier couldn't think of a single thing to say. "She is so beautiful. Damn, God did good."

Emiko bowed her head. Xavier had whispered what he thought he had kept in his own head. Her stomach flipped like it had last night, scaring her again. She had such a strong reaction to this man.

"We should go before Max calls and has a cow all over the place." Sam said stepping towards the door.

Emiko looked up, confused. "A cow?" she asked.

"It means before he gets very upset and worried," Sam clarified.

"Oh," she said with a single head nod.

The ride to Max's was long and quiet. Xavier had opted to give Emiko shotgun. He sat in the middle so that he could watch her in the rearview mirror. Every so often Sam and Xavier's eyes would meet, and Xavier would look away before Sam would get the courage to say something.

When they finally pulled up at Max's, there were about eight cars in the driveway.

"I thought it was just going to be us," Xavier said nervously. "I don't do groups well," the frightened man said quietly in shame.

"It's fine. People tend to hang in their comfort groups at Max's."

"I don't think I can do this, Sam. Call Max and tell him I'll see him in the office or something or I..."

"Xavier, you will be fine, we will be there for you," Emiko said as she turned to watch the Marine's face. "I am scared, too; I do not want to be alone with these people. I do not know them either."

She reached between the seats and lay her small hand on his knee "We will be all right together."

"Like I said before, strong," Xavier commented.

Emiko blushed.

"We good to go, Xavier?" Sam asked.

"Just don't put the keys away man. I'll see how long I can stay. I don't care how much these people have gone through, what they've seen or dealt with; I don't want to lose it in front of them. Can't really; I know too much that no one else can know."

"Need to know," Sam said questioningly.

"Yeah, this is not a good idea. This, I…"

Emiko's hand squeezed his knee reminding him that she was there to help. "We will not let anything happen to you," she said with much more confidence then she felt.

"Come on, before I chicken out again," He slid out the passenger's side door. This put the Jimmy between him and the house. A quick glance over his shoulder proved no one was behind him. Emiko touched his wrist and he stopped the jump that started, but she felt it. Quietly as if to herself, she started to sing her lullaby in Japanese again. Xavier took her hand and listened to her sing. He knew he could do this if she was there…he *hoped* he could do this if she was there.

He swallowed hard and nodded his head towards the house. "Let's go."

Sam walked up the steps ahead of the couple. He figured Xavier would need time to get himself together. He watched the young man glance around, knowing his friend was looking for anyone who might attack or, in this case, just plain startle him. The wind carried Emiko's voice enough that Sam could tell she was singing the nanny song again. She had started when Xavier almost jumped when she touched his hand. He saw the shattered boy nod and walk toward him with a look of utter desperation and total terror on his face.

The cop hoped that this would help
and not hinder his friend. Most of the time
Xavier looked his twenty-nine years, but
right now he looked like he had before he
joined the Corps. Sam hurt thinking about
what the world had done to such a strong
young man. He was angry that people
could treat each other with such hate, that
they could literally shatter a person's mind
but not their bodies, not enough for them
to die and escape their daily torture. He
knew Xavier was strong enough bodily to
keep living, but if they didn't find a way to
mend his soul soon he would do
something to end his life.

When Xavier was at the bottom
step Sam turned and pushed the doorbell,
knowing no one would hear the knock. He
heard the *bell* Max had put in for these
parties. It was P!nk's song "Get This Party
Started" that played.

When Xavier heard it play loudly,
he couldn't help but laugh. "Max is
seriously messed up, isn't he?"

"No more than anyone else,"
Crystal said as she opened the door.
"Samuel, Xavier, and you must be Emiko,"
Crystal nodded at each of the men and

pulled Emiko into a hug. "Welcome to the nut house. The men are out back, burning flesh. The women are in the living room playing with the little ones."

Crystal pointed toward the back of the house and started to pull Emiko toward the living room.

Max stepped into the house through the open screen door "Emiko, dear I want you to come and sing your beautiful song for a friend of mine. He hasn't heard it for a long time. He says he can't remember the words."

Emiko had not let go of Xavier's hand yet but had stepped toward Crystal, not knowing how to tell her hostess she would not leave her friend. Xavier and Sam started to tell Crystal that Emiko couldn't go with her, but Max saved them with his request.

"Oh, well you can come see the babies in a bit then, Emiko. Maybe you can sing to them, too."

Emiko bowed her head and replied, "Hai."

Max watched Xavier's face for a reaction to Emiko's use of Japanese but saw only a small flicker that was too fast to see.

Max one-arm hugged Sam and said, "Come on, old man, let's find a beer and flesh," He shouted "flesh" so that Crystal could hear it in the living room.

"You're not getting any" drifted out of the room in a sing song response.

"She always says that when I eat steak but I always do anyway."

"TMI man," Sam laughed.

Max laughed and dropped his arm off Sam's shoulder. He bent and pulled a few beers from the cooler next to the grill. He handed one to Sam, offered one to Xavier who took it and offered the last to Emiko, who declined.

"No, thank you."

"There's wine inside if you would prefer."

"Maybe later," she answered.

"Okay, just let me know if you change your mind. Guys, let me introduce you to Michael Soto," Max led the threesome toward an older Asian man sitting in the shade with sunglasses on. "Michael was one of my first patients."

"Michael, this is Sam, Xavier, and Emiko. I was telling you about the song she was singing yesterday for us," Max said loudly. He pointed toward his own ear and shook his head hoping the trio would understand Michael was hard of hearing; they all nodded their heads letting him know they did understand.

"Anatane oiė dekte, SotoSama," (I'm glad to see you Mr. Soto (with great respect) Emiko said and even thought he couldn't see her she bowed deeply from the waist.

"Au koto ga dekite totemo ureshii desu. Ogenki desu-ka?" (I am very glad to meet you. How are you?) Michael replied bowing slightly while seated.

Emiko glanced at Xavier to make sure he was still all right with the Japanese as had been spoken, but she saw his eyes were glazed over and unfocused. She reached out and touched his arm. He shook his head and smiled weakly at Emiko.

Max watched the interaction between the young couple. He had spent the night reading St. Cloud's and his teammates' files. He now knew about their

163 | P a g e

mission and what they had endured and, more importantly right now, what had been done to Xavier. Since Xavier's rescue, a few of his captor's underlings had been captured and questioned, so there was more information about the torture sessions that Xavier had endured than he could remember.

"Michael would love to hear the song, Emiko," Max gently pushed.

Xavier squeezed her hand when she shyly looked to him.

She sat down on the ground next to Michael's leg and began to sing for him. When she finished he wiped a tear from his eye and thanked her.

"Max," he said, "where is your beautiful wife? I think I would like to rest for a bit."

"I'm right here Michael, I figured it was about time to get you away from these heathens. Come on before they pollute you with their flesh-eating ways." With moves that showed how often Crystal helped the blind man, she walked him into the house and disappeared up the stairs. Sam followed her into the house and he disappeared too.

"Thank you, Emiko. Michael has been alone for a long time and has missed his homeland, but health conditions keep him from traveling."

She stood and bowed her head. "I would like a glass of wine now, please."

"No problem, be right back," Max went into the house and returned quickly with a glass of white zinfandel.

"Here you go, Emiko."

"Thank you."

"Shall we sit down?" Max pointed to the empty chairs away from most of the groups.

"Don't you need to, you know, circulate?" Xavier asked stalling.

"No, they are used to me staying with one or two people during these. They are here to just relax and be away from home for a few hours," The trio sat in chairs near a bubbling fountain in a back corner of the yard. "So how did it go last night?" Emiko blushed and turned away from Max, and Xavier coughed and cleared his throat and fidgeted. "Did something happen?"

"No, not really," Xavier said evasively.

"What does 'no, not really' include?"

"Sleep," Xavier answered.

"Then why the evasiveness?"

"We slept together."

"Sleep sleep or…"

"Yes, sleep, damn it," Xavier spat out, exasperation showing in his voice. "Why does everyone think we had sex? We just…" the frustrated man trailed off.

"Comforted each other," Emiko finished when Xavier could not.

"Any nightmares?" Max asked calmly.

"No."

"Yes," Emiko said quietly.

Max looked between the two, "You slept well Xavier?"

"As soon as my head hit the pillow."

"Emiko?"

"I slept well until this morning."

"I left her to answer the door for Sam, and when I came back she was rocking back and forth in the bed. She thought her dad had come to take me away."

"Emiko, if your father does come, you don't have to go with him. Just remember that, and he can't take anyone else with him either."

"I was worried when I woke and Xavier was gone..."

"I tried to wake you but it seems you're a very heavy sleeper," Xavier said, then poked her in the leg.

"I usually sleep lightly."

"Hmm," Max said, "Well you both had a very hard day yesterday. Do you think you can handle it here, Xavier?"

The Marine shrugged at the question. "We'll take it minute by minute and see how it goes. I won't let these people see me like I was yesterday. I can't let them."

"Pride?" Max asked knowing that wasn't how Xavier would answer, but unsure of what he would say.

"Security clearance."

CHAPTER SEVENTEEN

Max chuckled, "Ok, I'll buy that."

"What did you want me to say?"

"I wanted you to say exactly what you said. If you hide from me or tell me what you think I want to hear, this can't and won't work. I think you have reached a place where you know you can't keep going on this way and that you can't go back to what was before Afghanistan. If you want to, you will be able to bring enough of who you were with you. However, you have to leave the person you've been for three years behind."

"I don't know what I want anymore. For so long it was the three of us against, well, the world. Whether it was as kids against the parent's world, or the outside teenage world and then the big bad world itself, it was always US. We never," Xavier stopped to figure out how to say what he wanted to say, "there was never anything between the three of us, we were never a..."

Max held up his hand and said, "I understand."

"Ok, but we were as close as brothers could get. Hell, I don't think if we had been triplets we could have been closer. Though, um, bad thought considering how those two felt about each other."

"I get it," Max smiled and chuckled lightly, "you were in and through each other's lives, so much that they were and are a huge part of you."

"It was never I or me; it was always we and us," Xavier was starting to shake, the emotions becoming too much to handle.

Max could see the signs of stress showing. Xavier was shaking, fidgeting, and alternating between rubbing his hand over the back of his neck, over his face and through his hair. The Marine wore it longer than regulation, but it was still short enough that when he carded his fingers through it Max could see some of the scars on his scalp.

Xavier tipped his head back, closed his eyes against the blue sky above him, and tried to count over and over in his head. Closing his eyes had been a bad idea though, because as soon as he did, he saw

Lance and Shawn together the last time before they were taken. The trio had camped out to avoid running into someone and blowing their cover before it had started. There were some ruins of an old town; they were looking for water, and checking the perimeter. Lance and Shawn had gone left, Xavier had gone right. He came around a corner and found them kissing and hugging, looking content and happy. He made noise as he came around the corner breaking the couple apart. "Sorry man, got turned around somehow."

The two had laughed at him; Xavier never got turned around. They knew they had been dawdling and that he had done most of the work. Xavier wished to every god, higher power or whomever, every day that he could have left them there, forever in love and safe.

Max watched Xavier's internal struggle and knew he was losing, could see the emotional pain turned into physical pain on his face. Emiko could see it, too. Max raised his hand to get Emiko's attention. When she looked at him, he tipped his head to Xavier and reached out his hand.

Emiko understood that Max wanted her to help Xavier, but she was not sure how to do it. Careful not to startle him, she reached over and laid her hand on his cheek. She hummed the little lullaby and smiled when Xavier's face stopped contorting in pain and he nuzzled her hand.

"Xavier, what were you thinking about just then?" Max asked softly.

"It was about the last night before hell opened up and swallowed us."

Emiko could not stop herself from asking, "Was it happy?"

Xavier nodded once, "But it hurts."

"Why does it hurt, Xavier?" Max wondered.

Xavier shuddered and desperately tried to control the emotion in his voice when he answered, "Because they will never be that happy again."

"Of course they will. Do you believe in heaven or reincarnation?"

Shrugging he replied, "I suppose so."

"Either way, they will find each other."

Emiko wondered if Cassandra could find them. She had heard the other girls talk about what Cassandra could see and feel. Emiko was not sure this would be within her abilities; she would ask the next time she saw the witch and then ask Xavier if he would want to know.

"Will you tell me why they were happy?" Max asked.

"A few stolen minutes where they didn't have to hide," After a long pause he continued, "We had camped in some old ruins; they went to do a perimeter check, watching for water along the way. I went the other direction. They took a few minutes to just be. I walked up on them just hugging and kissing and they were…"

"Happy," Max finished when Xavier stopped and couldn't. "Are you jealous that they had each other and you didn't have anyone?"

"No, God no, I would never have wished that on anyone. They were there for me as much as I was for them. Hell, when we were cold and couldn't light a fire because it would give away our position, we would put our bags together and sleep together. They always stuck me in the middle. Both of them were infernos when they slept and I was generally cold no matter what. We had to put some physical comfort ahead of everything else because if you get sick out there you're going to die and it increases the chances that your team will, too."

"You know that you should have never been put on a team together. You guys should have been broken up because of your childhood relationship, especially because of their relationship, even though no one knew about it, because if..."

"If an enemy had seen their relationship, they could have and would have used it against them and our country," Xavier interrupted Max with a look that could kill. "Yes, I know."

"Xavier, if you guys had been broken up and they had died separately, do you think you would still have this survivors' guilt or do you think you would be able to accept their deaths for what they were - a sacrifice for the country they loved?"

CHAPTER EIGHTEEN

Xavier sat for a very long time. He wasn't sure how to answer the question; it hadn't been asked before. No one had thought of the situation that way before, because no one ever knew the whole situation. He was at a total loss.

"Xavier..." Max said hoping he hadn't fried the man's brain with his question.

"I don't know, I need to think about..." waving his hand trying to show the abstractness of the situation.

Glancing at his watch, Max said, "It's about time for me to start grilling. Do you want to stay here or would you prefer to go into the house?"

"Here for now, I think."

"Okay, I doubt anyone will come over and disturb you, but if someone does, just let them know you would prefer to be alone." Max patted Xavier on the leg before walking off to fire up the grill.

"Emiko, you don't have to stay with me. You can go in with the babies if you want."

"No, I said I would not leave you. I will not."

"You are so sweet, but there is no reason for you to stay with me. I'll be fine; I just want to think for a bit."

"I like staying with you," she said.

"Emiko, I love it that you want to be here with me, but you are very distracting."

Emiko's face fell. "I, I am, I, I am sorry." She hurried to get up, but Xavier stopped her from rushing off before he could explain.

"No, no, that's not what I meant, damn it. I keep putting my foot in it," There was a break in the hedge that appeared to lead down a small path; he pulled Emiko through the hedge.

He stopped when they were far enough down the path that no one could see them from the break. "Emiko, you don't understand what you do to me. You can't understand. You make me crazy, crazy-crazy even. Not sad crazy but *'I want to pin you to the nearest surface and make love to you for hours crazy'*. Since I met you three days ago, my world has gone upside down. And considering how out of whack it was before, that's saying something. Yesterday before my little trip to hell, I actually thought for a few seconds about taking you back to my apartment and trying to convince you that I'm a worthy person, that I would be good enough for you.

In the last three days, I have thought more times about the future than I have in the last three years. Since I woke up that day, I haven't been able to think about tomorrow because I didn't want a tomorrow. I only wanted yesterday to be a nightmare, so that when I woke up it would be over and my best friends wouldn't be dead, my brothers would be there to tell me I'm losing it and to go get laid. But they really are gone, and I still can't quite deal with it. When I say you're distracting, it's because I go back to those thoughts of wanting to find the nearest bed and make you scream my name, but you deserve so much more than I could ever give you."

She was so confused; Emiko didn't know what to do. No one in her family had ever acted like her feelings and opinions mattered. She was just there and would do what she was told to do, would do what needed to be done. It had hurt being called a distraction, but she didn't understand why. She had no claim on Xavier. She could never have a claim on him. As much as Xavier tried to say he was not worthy, she felt she was the unworthy one. Her family would certainly agree with her. Everyone here in the States had been telling her that her family was unworthy of her, not the other way around, but she had too many years of family honor drummed into her to stop thinking that her family was right and that her new friends were wrong.

"If you keep looking so sad and lost, I'm going to have to kiss you 'till you look happy and dazed."

Emiko's head snapped up and she looked at Xavier's eyes. They were huge but showing almost none of their beautiful dark grey. Instead, she found herself lost in a black pool rimmed by silver moonlight. She shook her head and stepped back, when her back hit the tree she stopped and said breathlessly, "I want you to, but I am afraid still."

"I won't hurt you."

"I never thought you would; I am afraid that I will not be enough and you will..." she could not finish her thought, more afraid that speaking it would bring her worst fear to life.

"I'm not going to go away, Emiko. I don't, I know, I, crap, this is crazy. I don't think I can leave you. Shit, this sounds like one of those romance books Louise was always reading. I haven't even known you a week yet and I know that I can't live without you. You have changed my life in so many ways in such a short time. I see light for the first time in years, and you're in the middle of it. The light starts with you, Emiko."

Emiko blushed, nothing started with her. She was not worthy of being the beginning of something. "I am here to be your friend, to be what you need, but I am not a light," she whispered.

"You are a light, Emiko. You are my light, trust me, I've been in the dark. I know when I see the opposite." Xavier stepped closer to Emiko, pinning her to the tree so she couldn't get away from him. She would have to hear what he wanted to say. "I can see a tomorrow with you; I want to see a tomorrow with you. I NEED to see it with you," he said, pulling her into an embrace. He leaned his head on her shoulder and whispered in her ear, "I haven't felt the need for anything but a bullet in three years, Emiko."

They both shivered at his confession. "It has scared me for three years. I wanted it so bad; I would sit on my bed for hours, staring at my gun, the gun that killed my friends. I would pull the trigger back just far enough, but not too far. I would sit that way for hours, hoping my finger would twitch enough to make it fire but in three years it never did. The day before yesterday was the first time since I was released from the hospital that I didn't sit and wait for the gun to go off. Last night was the first night that I didn't drink myself to the point of passing out just to be able to sleep. Last night is the first night that I didn't have at least six nightmares. Last night I had no nightmares, last night I had no dreams, nothing. With you in my arms, you in my bed, last night is the first time I *slept*."

Emiko was shaking for so many reasons, very few of which she could actually name. She was scared to think of what would have happened if she had never met this man, and she was sure her life would have stopped that day in the alley. She was shaking because she could feel the loss of his friends, his sorrow at the separation from them, and the guilt he carried thinking that he should have been able to do something. She also felt the need to kiss him and to let him take control of her body and do what he wanted.

"Xavier, the day you stopped that man you did not save my life."

Xavier stepped back confused and was starting to become angry at what she had said, but Emiko stepped to him, placed a hand on his heart, and continued, "You did not save my life because it did not begin until you carried me to the couch. Until I stood up to the thief, I had never done anything for me, solely for me. Everything I had done until that moment was for other people or survival."

"I would say trying to get yourself stabbed is not the best way to survive."

"I did not care. I only wanted *not* to do what he said. I wanted just once to be my own person and to tell someone else 'no'."

Dropping his head so that it rested on the top of Emiko's, Xavier whispered, "Next time don't try it with someone who has a knife on you."

"I am sure Cassandra's fates meant for us to be where we were that day. I am sure I need you as much as you need me."

"Do you think Max would be upset if we bailed and went to my apartment? I think we need to be alone," Xavier asked the rhetorical question because whether Max cared or not, they were going.

Emiko blushed again and raised her shoulders. Letting them fall, she swallowed before she could speak again. "What about Sam?"

"Screw Sam, he can find his own ride home."

CHAPTER NINETEEN

Max had almost felt like a voyeur each time it looked like Xavier was going to kiss Emiko, but Max needed to know if Xavier would open up to Emiko about his feelings. The psychiatrist knew Xavier might never tell the girl what happened to him during his capture, but then he really didn't need to. Xavier needed Emiko to stay naive and innocent of how much the world could hurt people. Xavier needed her to remember that there were still good people in the world. Walking back to the yard as quietly as he had walked away from it, he was glad Sam had come back out; he needed to let the cop know he was about to be wheel-less.

"Sam, uh, hate to tell you this, but you are about to get ditched."

"Huh?" Sam said turning around to find Max right behind him with a shit eating grin.

"Was doing a little recon and have some intel that says in about two minutes Xavier is going to come and ask for your keys and hope like hell you can get a ride back to town."

"Recon, intel… is that spook for eavesdropping on patients?"

"Sure, why not."

Sam laughed and saw Xavier and Emiko come through a break in the hedge. Seeing the look on Xavier's face made Sam's heart unclench and his shoulders straighten a bit. Xavier looked almost happy; there was almost a light in his eyes again. The shadows that seemed to live under his eyes almost looked lighter, the cloud that had hung over the man for years almost looked smaller and less dark. Sam almost saw the boy he knew return to the man he was coming to know. He really hoped that someday soon his friend would be happy, instead of almost.

"Need your keys, old man," Xavier demanded when he walked up to Sam.

"You do, huh? You got a license to drive, kid?"

"You should know, copper, you taught me to drive."

"Nope, only taught you to drive in a pursuit."

"Same diff, keys."

"And what makes you think I'm going to let you strand me out at the old guy's place? He snores loud enough to wake the dead."

"I resent that remark."

"No you resemble it and you know it."

Xavier laughed at the older men and their attempt to play the tension down. "Give me the keys, Sam, or I'll hot wire the fucker, and Max can give you a ride home as punishment for spying on us. Not a very good spook." Xavier said looking from Max to Sam making sure both men got that he knew they had been talking about him. Also wanting Max to know he had been caught without even knowing it. "If you're going to do recon, don't come around smelling like steak and Drakkar."

Sam laughed and fished his keys out of his pocket. "Don't wrap it around a telephone pole, please. I'll have the wife come get me."

"You keep calling her that and she'll be the ex-wife," Max told him.

"Nope, she never hears about it."

CHAPTER TWENTY

In the truck on the way home, Xavier wouldn't let go of Emiko's hand, his thumb never stopped rubbing the back of it. He was getting nervous; the 40-minute ride to his apartment was giving him too much time. He was trying to talk himself out of this, but he was sure if he did, he would hurt Emiko, and that was what he was trying to avoid.

Pulling into the parking lot of a pharmacy a few blocks from his complex, he turned off the Jimmy and looked at Emiko. Her head was so low her chin rested on her chest. She was trembling slightly and there was a blush across her cheeks.

"Emiko," Xavier said "I, are you sure you want to do this?"

Her head nodded once and the blush grew. "I do not know what to do, though," she said just above a whisper.

"You don't have to do anything, sweetie." He reached over and ran his hand across her cheek. He moved her hair so that he could see all of her profile. "You are so beautiful." Xavier took a deep breath to ask the question he had to ask. He moved his hand under her chin, lifted her face up, and turned it toward him. "Are you on any birth control?" He felt his own cheeks flush at being so blunt, but he was fairly sure Emiko wouldn't get it if he said, "So are we good or do I need to go in there?'

She shook her head once. "No," she whispered.

"Okay, I will be right back. I, we, I, crap, no kids right now," he said sliding out of the truck, "maybe someday."

Emiko stayed in the truck unsure of anything. She knew she wanted this, she thought she knew that Xavier wanted this. She just really did not know how to do this. She had to admit she knew the basics; her au pair had told her about some of "the birds and the bees" as Melissa called it. She just did not know what he would expect of her. Before she could get anymore scared, Xavier was back with a small brown bag and was blushing more than when he had left. Dropping the bag between them on the seat he started the truck and made it to his apartment building in three minutes "Stay," he said grabbing the bag.

Emiko was getting tired of being confused so much of the time. Then her door opened and Xavier carefully pulled her from the truck and carried her up the stairs. At his door, he set her on her feet, unlocked the door, and picked her up again.

He didn't stop until he reached his room and his bed. He knelt on the corner and laid her down as he had last night. She lay there looking up at him, her eyes the color of rich chocolate. Xavier could see her trying to control her fear and trembling. Dropping the bag to the floor, he knelt with one leg on each side of her. He slid his jacket off and dropped it to the floor. Then slowly he un-zipped her sweater and pulled it off her left arm, then her right. He carefully tugged it out from underneath her.

Emiko's breathing became more shallow and faster. Xavier smiled and leaned down, kissing her cheek near her eye, then the middle of her forehead, next her other cheek at the corner of her other eye. He kissed her nose and he heard her breath slow and deepen more. Rubbing her nose with his, he tilted her head until he could kiss her lips, just a simple kiss, one on each corner. Then he kissed her chin, he heard Emiko sigh and her breathing slow just a little more. Now that he was sure she wouldn't hyperventilate when he kissed her, he did. She moaned into the kiss and when he traced her lips with his tongue, she opened her mouth just a little. Xavier's tongue slid in and he felt Emiko shudder and rise up to brush against his groin. He groaned at the contact with his hard cock. He hadn't been this hard in so long, long enough he didn't want to dwell on it. He only hoped to God he wouldn't embarrass himself and come before he was actually in Emiko.

Feeling Emiko's tongue tentatively touch his made Xavier sigh, however girlie that sounded. He felt her hand on the small of his back caressing him. He smiled into the kiss.

Emiko thought she was getting the hang of this kissing business; she made sure to mimic whatever he did. When she tried to trace his lips as he had hers and her tongue had touched his, a spark leapt in her stomach. Then when he sighed, she was sure she was doing it right. She wanted to feel more of him, she moved her hand up toward his back and over his shirt, and her stomach was tight again.

Xavier growled when she moved her hand back down towards his ass and he deepened the kiss, again pressing his tongue into her mouth. Emiko sucked in a breath and tried to do the same thing but Xavier wasn't having any of that. He wanted the control. He moved and grabbed both of her hands, sliding them out and up on the bed. When he had both hands caught in his left hand over her head, he slid his right hand down. He found the edge of her shirt and slid his hand under it, until he found her breast. Finding her nipple hard he grinned again and growled immediately as she bucked under him. "Emiko," he whispered breaking the kiss only to move to her ear. Her sharp intake of breath made Xavier laugh into her ear, "My little one, you haven't felt nothing yet," he murmured to her.

As he undid each button, he would glide the back of his finger across her silky skin to the next button. With the last button, he caressed up to her cheek, moving over to her shoulder and up her arm. Exchanging hands, he used his left to trace down her arm to her cheek and then to her breast. He returned to kissing her to distraction. He let go of her hands figuring she would leave them there and pulled her shirt free. When he felt for the zipper on her skirt and found it, he slowly unzipped it and began sliding it down her soft legs. Emiko moaned as he tugged it past her hips, and he felt her lift her hips a little so he could push it down more. Kneeling on only one leg, he used his foot to pull her skirt the rest of the way off kicking it to the floor with the rest of the clothes.

Breaking the kiss, he leaned back and sucked in his own breath. Emiko was beautiful, the jade green bra and panties looked perfect against her dark skin. Her hair was mussed enough to show anyone who looked that she had been kissed well. The tinge of pink in her cheeks made her look even more innocent. "Emiko, I, I, I can't tell you... I have no words, you are perfect." He kissed her on the nose again. Lying next to her on the bed, he kissed her lips as he rolled her to her side facing him. Being self-conscious still about his scars Xavier was still fully dressed, but he had an idea of how to distract her from noticing them when he had to shed his clothes.

Xavier caressed Emiko's back, sliding his hand lower with each caress when he reached her leg, he slid her leg over his hip and draped it there; he kept kissing her and rubbing one hand along her back and one hand over her leg. When Emiko arched her back pressing their groins together, Xavier slipped his hand back up her leg and slid his fingers under the leg band of her panties.

Emiko stiffened for a second when she felt Xavier's hand on her skin; she was startled, and confused, but all thoughts left her mind when he nibbled on her ear again. This time she didn't react when his other hand unhooked her bra, letting her breasts free. Nor did she react when she felt him slip one strap off gently, lifting her up so that the other could be removed. His lips left her ear and found their way to her shoulder, right where it met with her neck. She arched hard as she gasped in pleasure.

Xavier took the opportunity while she was distracted to add her panties to the floor.

Emiko shivered as her last remaining clothes were removed, but she was too wrapped up in her feelings to take note that Xavier was still fully dressed, including his boots.

Xavier rolled Emiko onto her back and pushed her leg outward so he could rub the inside of her thigh. Making small circles with one hand, each one edging just a bit higher than the last and caressing the side of her breast with the other hand, Xavier kept Emiko under a haze of lust until she was excited enough to allow instinct to take over and to just react.

He knew she was ready for the next step when her hands began to wander on their own, one joining his on her breast, the other reaching up to rest on his neck. Xavier moved his hand from her thigh to her stomach and glided it down to her outer lips. She moaned and gasped at that first ghost of a touch. When Xavier raised his hand to trace the path over again Emiko lifted her hips from the bed. Xavier swallowed hard and dipped one finger into her pussy. Emiko shuddered and gasped again, lazily he slid it up and over her clit.

Emiko cried out at the sudden pleasure that ripped through her body. Xavier touched her again and waves of pleasure surged through her again, she felt him slip into her again using his thumb to rub "that place" again, and then she felt a second finger and the world exploded. "Xavier!" she screamed.

Xavier couldn't help but smile wide while he watched Emiko orgasm, calling his name. He had told her she would scream his name. Xavier stayed by her helping her ride her first orgasm until the bitter end. When she finally stopped writhing on the bed, he slid off and undid his boots, kicking them off quickly, followed by his socks, pants, and underwear. His shirt was the last to land on the floor in the growing pile of fabrics. Xavier realized that Emiko was coming back to herself a little faster than he wanted, grabbing the bag from under her shirt, Xavier dumped out the box and tore it open. Pulling a condom loose, he ripped it open and rolled it on his hard cock. He hissed as the sensation ripped through him, damn near making him come. *"You moron you're going to fuck this up, you're never going to last."* Taking a deep breath and holding onto the base of his cock almost to the point of pain, he waited until he wasn't on the verge of coming.

Emiko's eyes fluttered open to see Xavier's face looking tormented. Instantly she was afraid she had done something to trigger another flashback for him. She reached up to touch his arm but then he shuddered and looked down at her. Before she could say a word he was kissing her senseless again. Emiko could do nothing but shudder and moan. Xavier's hand returned to her pussy and two fingers found their way into her again and she cried out again. As soon as she did, Xavier pushed into her quickly and stopped when he felt the pop. He heard her cry of pain and he held her. "I'm sorry, I had to. It won't hurt anymore, though. It's okay."

Emiko stiffened at the pain but as Xavier held her and soothed her, she relaxed again.

"Are you okay?" He asked her.
"Yes."

"Good." He kissed her again, relaxing her more. When she kissed him back, he started with small short strokes, pausing after each one to make sure she was still all right.

Emiko wanted more. More what, she so did not know but there was something. Xavier was teasing her with the way he was moving. Each time he moved, she felt it, the something getting closer, but he would stop and it would flutter away. The next time he stopped, she moved with him and her clit rubbed against his pelvis. She moaned and sighed, the feeling stayed this time.

Xavier smiled to himself, and he didn't pause his strokes this time. Figuring she wouldn't think of it, he wrapped her legs around his waist. This tilted her differently and when he thrust in, she cried out in surprise at the newer feeling it caused. Smiling yet again, he picked up the pace. With every stroke, Emiko cried out again and again. He felt her orgasm building, her inner muscles quivering, pulling him closer to his own release. Not sure how much longer he could hold on, he reached between them finding her clit.

Rubbing it with his finger again, she came immediately taking him with her.

They both yelled the other's name as they convulsed around one another.

CHAPTER TWENTY-ONE

Xavier came for what seemed like hours, when he finally stopped he dropped to the side of Emiko, making sure not to crush her. He wanted to make sure she was okay but words wouldn't form, so he lay there for a moment, trying to get blood flow back to the upper brain so he could speak.

Emiko panted heavily as she recovered from her orgasm. For the first time in her life, she felt good, really good. Turning her head so she could see Xavier, she laughed a little to herself. "I thought that was a myth," she said very quietly. Xavier was lying on his stomach, asleep. She giggled but when she did, it moved the bed a little bit, and something caught her attention, something on Xavier's back. Gingerly she reached over and traced the mate to the scar that she had seen in the restaurant.

Sitting up a bit she gasped when she saw all of the scars on his back, there were dozens. She was leaning on one arm and her other was over her mouth in horror of what this wonderful man had had to endure. As a tear rolled down her cheek, it was caught.

"Don't," the one word had so many emotions in it.

"Oh, Xavier why would…"

"Don't," he said sitting up, his chest bearing fewer noticeable scars.

"I am sorry, I did not mean to make you think of…"

"No, Emiko." Xavier pulled the sheet over his lap but then pulled her into his lap and held her. "Maybe someday I can talk about them, but this is about you today, not me."

"I would like for it to be about us."

"I, okay I can deal with that, but I can't talk about those, not now. I need more time in your light," he murmured, nuzzling her neck. "I am going to go get a washcloth to clean us up a little, then we can have a nap and we can do that all over again, if you're up to it."

Emiko moaned and blushed; she nodded once trying not to be bashful but failing.

Setting her down on the bed and laughing, Xavier walked to the bathroom.

Finding a washcloth while the water warmed up, he disposed of the condom, though he was sure most of what it had held was on the bed. Guess they could sleep on top of the sheet with the comforter for their little nap.

Looking in the mirror while he wrung out the washcloth, he swallowed back memories of how he got each scar. Not all of his scars were from his capture. There were ten small scars from a shotgun blast that while painful as hell, hadn't done any real damage. The scar on his right arm was from a knife that went through but missed everything vital. The docs had told him he was a lucky fucker for that one and the one on his hip. He had been lucky; some jungle chick had thought he needed to lose a bit, by way of her machete. She mostly missed; well, she missed the really important parts. His right knee, that scar was fun. Rock climbing for fun and he slips like a recruit and slices his leg open on a chunk of shale. Then there was the damned horse that had kicked him in the left leg. He had been far enough back to end up with a scar and crutches for a month. The last of the non-capture scars were on his left forearm. They had been trying to get out of South America quickly and he gotten tangled up in razor wire. If he thought about it, he had made it, scratched but mostly unhurt, from every op he'd gone on.

Least with the last one, he had plenty of scars to show for the hell he had lived though. Going back to Emiko, he told her to lie back. Careful not to scare her he cleaned her and got rid of the cloth.

"Are you hungry or tired?" he asked.

"Sleepy, a little."

Xavier lay next to her and pulled her to him. Both of them lying on their left sides, he had his arms wrapped around her as she snuggled up to him, pressing her ass right into his groin.

"You keep doing that, little one, and we are not going to be sleeping." He chuckled as she went board stiff. "Oh little one, you are good for me; you make me laugh."

CHAPTER TWENTY-TWO

Emiko relaxed again, snuggling in close to Xavier-chan. She wrinkled her nose. The traditional way of showing endearment in Japan was to add chan to the end of a name, but with Xavier, it sounded wrong. Saver-chan sounded only slightly better, but she didn't like either version. Mildly she thought of something else she could call him. Idly she began tracing the scar on his arm, back and forth. Her eyes would droop, pop back open, and then droop farther 'til finally she dropped off to sleep.

Some time close to sunset Emiko woke up but she was not sure why. She stretched a little to work out a few kinks, but when she relaxed back into koishii-chan she yelped in surprise. His erection had poked her in the butt cheek and startled her.

Coming awake in a second to see why Emiko had yelled he blinked a few times. "Wha, what, where?" he said bleary eyed.

"Koishii-chan," she said and pointed down to his hard-on.

"Huh, what?"

"You poked me," she giggled.

"Oh, well I poked you earlier and you didn't say anything," he said flipping her on to her back and pinning her to the bed, "now did you?"

"No, koishii-chan."

"What is that?"

"What is what?" she said confused.

"That word you keep calling me, I thought chan was for little kids."

"Sometimes it is used between close friends and family."

"So what is the koi ko she thing," he said, trying to pronounce the word she had used.

"Koishii means beloved or wanted."

"Hmm, I can live with that."

"Xavier-chan did not sound very nice; neither did Saver-chan."

"Hmm," Xavier shivered, Emiko was running her hand over his back, and he was trying not to think about *them.* "Emiko, stop, please."

"You do not like koishii-chan? I, I thought yo..."

"No, the name is fine. Don't, my back, I…" he said, emotions strangling his voice.

Her hand stopped instantly, dropping to the bed. She tried to tip her head down in shame for forgetting his dislike of the marks but only managed to bump her head into his.

"No, don't hide; you didn't do anything wrong. I'm just not ready for that yet," he murmured, nudging her head back up. "Don't hide," he said again, when he could look her in the eyes. "Maybe someday I won't remember that they are there, but for now," kissing her lightly "please don't."

"Gomen nasai, koishii-chan."

"Uhhh, hun, I really only speak a few words. I have no idea what you just said."

"I am sorry koishii-chan, I forget when I get upset, and I speak…"

"It's fine. I'm still here, I didn't go anywhere this time."

"If you go away, I will sing you home."

Xavier smiled, touching their foreheads together. "Yes, you will. Are you hungry yet?"

"Some."

"Or would you rather…" leaving the statement unfinished Xavier scooted down on the bed so that he could reach her breast and he started sucking on her rapidly hardening nipples.

"Not so hungry," Emiko said, wondering if he would let her explore him. Kissing to the other breast, Xavier made Emiko gasp when his hand found its way between her legs.

"Koishii-chan!" she exclaimed. "I want to…"

He looked up, "You want to what, love?"

"I want to…" she said faltering. "See you," she finally whispered.

"Do you now?"

Emiko felt as if her cheeks had been put to a flame. "Yes," she answered his question after what seemed a lifetime.

"Well then I guess I should let you," Xavier replied after taking a steadying breath. He rolled them so that he was on the bottom and she was lying on his chest.

She hugged him and sat up. "You know what girls look like, more than one girl I would guess, but I do not…" trailing off, she stopped. She couldn't quite get the courage to say "I want to see *'your dangly bits'* as she had heard Melissa call it once.

"Yes, I have seen more than one woman and I know you haven't."

"I have seen lots of girls," she said light heartedly.

"Did you just joke with me?"

"I went to an all girl school, koishii-chan. I have seen more girls than you."

"You are joking with me."

"No, I really did go…," thinking her attempt at teasing was going very wrong; she was no good at it.

"I bet you did love," Xavier said while playing with her breasts. "Just what exactly did you see at this all girl school?"

"I saw…" she paused, to see if she remembered anything he might want to hear about.

"Hmm yeeees, what did you see? Did you see other girls kissing and…"

"No, no, oh no."

"No," he said sounding crushed. "No girls doing this?" he asked, reaching up and kissing her fully, then lying back on the bed. "Nothing like this?" he wondered, snaking his hand down to her pussy, easily sliding a finger into her. He watched her tip her head back, eyes closed. Leaning back up he sucked a diamond hard nipple into his mouth and nibbled just a little. "No girl on girl action, I'm disappointed."

"No, no, no," Emiko shook her head and batted at his, which was still attached to her breast. "I am supposed to get to see you. No distracting me, it is not fair. I cannot…" a sigh interrupted her when Xavier fought dirty and rubbed his thumb over her clit.

"No, no," she said, pulling herself back again, scooting away from him. "No fair you, oh, uh, you lie on your hands."

"What?" Xavier said innocently. "I wasn't doing anything."

"Yes you were. Put your hands under your head and, and, keep your lips to yourself."

"Do you really want that?" Xavier countered reaching out for her again.

"Please," she whispered again.

"Alright you win," Xavier said placing his hands under his head.

Swallowing hard, he tried to keep down the memories this position rekindled, but the look on Emiko's face pushed them all away.

CHAPTER TWENTY-THREE

Emiko had scooted back far enough on the bed that she could see his cock waving at full attention. Very slowly, she reached for him. With one finger, she touched the velvety skin on his cock. She traced the largest vein to the head then traced the cleft to the opening. Xavier groaned and she snatched her hand back.

"No, you're fine, more than fine, it feels good."

Emiko looked up and found Xavier's eyes almost black again, the vein in his neck as big as the one she had just followed and his body glistening with a light sheen of sweat. A little bolder Emiko moved up the bed reaching for him again, this time she wrapped her fingers around him causing him to moan, expecting it this time Emiko did not stop in her study of him.

She saw the scar on the hip across from her and her heart hurt again. Why him, why did this man have to bear so many reminders of his loss? But she did not want him to notice her looking at it so she closed her eyes and wondered if she was brave enough to kiss "it". Emiko may have been a virgin before today, but working with Melissa and the others had taught her many things...well, sort of. She knew certain things were done between a couple, but until now she was not sure how they worked out. Sneaking a quick glance at Xavier and finding his eyes closed, she decided to try, and leaning over, she kissed the tip very softly.

Xavier hissed, "Oh God."

"I did..."

"No, you did fine. Just didn't expect that, wasn't ready."

"Oh, so I..." an impish grin played across her lips.

"Yes, you can keep doing that," Xavier said, his eyes opening wide.

Emiko leaned over again but the way she was lying hurt her neck, so she sat up looking at him, wondering what would be a better way. She did not want to ask.

Xavier could guess what she was thinking but waited to see if she wanted help or if she would figure it out on her own. After a minute though, he gave up and slid to the middle of the bed. "Kneel across the bed," he told her, and he watched Emiko's cheeks go bright red but she did as he said. She hesitated when she saw that he was watching her, so he closed his eyes. A second later, he was rewarded with another fluttering kiss on his shaft.

Emiko slid her fingers around him and licked the tip. She smiled to herself when she heard Xavier hissing again. She took this sound to mean she was doing a good thing, even if it sounded like he was in pain. She moved her hand down his shaft to feel the golden brown hair that surrounded him. The hiss was followed quickly by a moan and his hips bucking up.

"Oh Emiko."

Figuring she had stumbled onto something very good, Emiko glided her hand back up to the top and slid it down again and was pleased to receive another moan. A term she heard Melissa use popped into her head: this was a hand job. And if she took him all the way in her mouth, that would be a blowjob, though from what little she did know, it was more sucking than blowing.

Feeling brave and more confident than she ever had, Emiko took a deep breath and slid Xavier into her mouth when her hand came up again.

"Emiko, oh God, you have no idea how good that feels, oh hell."

Trying to remember the things Melissa said were good to do, she curled her tongue and pulled up as her hand pulled down. She swirled her tongue around the edge and felt Xavier shiver and his cock grow harder. To keep her balance Emiko had put her hand between Xavier's legs next to his balls, she felt them twitch against her arm.

She jumped a little when she felt a hand on her back but was trying to concentrate on what she was doing so paid no mind to it. After a few minutes, though that hand was hard to ignore. It had pulled her so she was more facing the foot of the bed than the side and that hand was doing very wicked things to her. It would slip two fingers in and out a few times, then the thumb would swirl across her clit, making her shiver, and then everything would repeat all over again.

Emiko was finding it very hard to concentrate. She wanted to keep doing what she was doing, but she also wanted to concentrate on the feeling the hand was igniting. A few minutes more and the hand left her. She whimpered, but Xavier chuckled.

"Come here."

Turning to look at him, Xavier pulled her up even with him. "Your turn," he said flipping her to her back, making her cry out in surprise.

He kissed her once, then pushed her legs apart and kissed her pussy.

"Oh hai, oh oh, ooooh, I oh, koishii-chan," she sighed.

Xavier licked her juices clean and looked for more. As he slipped his tongue into her, he felt her tense and relax immediately. She was getting better at going with the flow when it came to sex. He sucked her clit in between his teeth, grazing it. She cried out and shuddered, but he was nowhere near done with her yet.

"Oh, princess."

Hoping to carry her further, he sucked her clit in again swirling his tongue around it and pressed two fingers into her. Emiko bucked once and screamed Xavier's name again. Quickly sliding into her, Xavier felt her orgasm all over his cock. Something's missing, he thought for half a second as he pushed all the way into her. Wanting to keep her on the edge, he moved immediately and kept the pace quick. Emiko soon was keeping his pace and writhing under him, calling his name over and over again. This time was not going to be much longer than the last. It had just been too long for him to have any stamina but he was going to work on that. Emiko came once again and he joined her.

Xavier woke a very short time later to a little snore in his ear; he looked down and found Emiko asleep under him. He smiled at how precious she looked. Lifting up off her, he reached to keep the condom from making a mess to find no condom at all.

"Fuck, fuck, fuck. Damn it, damn it."

Emiko stretched and whimpered a bit before saying sleepily, "What is wrong?"

"You said you weren't on the pill right?" he asked, hoping he was wrong and knowing damn good and well he wasn't.

"Yes, I am not on birth control," waking up a little more, "Why?"

"I, oh God, Emiko, what have I done?" he sat on the bed heavily, at the last second turning so his back was away from her.

Still sleep-dazed, Emiko did not understand what he meant. "I did something wrong? I was not..."

"No, no, oh God, no. Emiko you were so wonderful I forgot to put on a condom."

"I do not understand. I..." Emiko began, sitting up trying to grasp what seemed like a simple concept. "I, you, we are..."she babbled.

"Emiko, I could have gotten you pregnant." Seeing she was not going to get it, he smiled at her naiveté but wanted her to understand the problem.

It took that one statement for Emiko to wake all the way up. "Oh, oh," she said rather high-pitched. "Oh," her tone dropped several levels. "We will just have to wait and see koishii-chan," she said calmly. "I am hungry and a little sticky. Could we maybe shower and find something to eat?" she asked hopefully.

"You are not going to worry about this?"

"When it is time I may, but for now, no. There is little to be done right now."

"Okay." He picked her up from the bed and carried her into the bathroom. She giggled the whole way. He set her down on the cold toilet seat and she jumped up squealing. "Xavier, that is cold," she pouted.

"I know, it was payback for the giggling in my ear."

"Humph," Emiko continued to pout, bumping him with her hip when he bent over to straighten the bathmat; he almost lost his balance but caught himself.

"You little.. you're gonna get it now." Xavier reached for Emiko but she dodged out of the way and was out of the bathroom in a flash and into the living room. Emiko was not sure what she had started, but the playful look on Xavier's face was enough for her to want to keep the game going as long as she could. She jumped over the couch and landed lightly behind it, ducking down before he was able to scramble his way out of the little

215 | P a g e

room, and biting the inside of her cheek to keep from laughing.

"You're going to get it, little one. You had better come out, and I'll go easy on you," he called out laughing. "I'll only tickle you 'til you can't breathe." He knew her options were fairly limited: in the kitchen, behind the couch, or behind the chair. He sidestepped to the chair looking over the back, not finding her. He was sure she wouldn't go in the kitchen, knowing it would trap her. He stepped into it to check anyway.

Emiko saw Xavier step into the kitchen and she moved to the farthest side of the couch from the kitchen.

"Emiko, little Emiko, where oh where did she go? When I find her, I'm going to have to pin her to the cold floor and tickle her everywhere. Then I'm going to have to kiss her silly again but I think I already did that 'cause she's being awfully silly right now."

Emiko was biting her tongue so hard trying not to laugh and give away where she was. She paused when she heard a door in the kitchen open, she was not sure if it was the refrigerator or the freezer - either one did not bode well for her if she was caught. "Silly girl, come out and take it like a man." A little giggle came from the living room and then a gasp as she realized she had given away her position. Not that he had needed it; he was prolonging the capture for the sake of the game. He turned and heard little feet scamper out of the living room and back to the bathroom and the door shut.

"Oh little one, we will have to teach you how to play hide and seek," he said to himself, walking to the bathroom. He heard her giggling like a loon on the other side of the door. Knowing the lock on the door didn't work, he opened the door and got a cup of cold water in the face. "Oh you really are gonna get it now, missy."

He stepped dripping into the bathroom and shut the door behind him. He took one step to her and wrapped his arm around her waist to keep her still, then put the other hand, full of ice chips, to her breast making her squeal loudly.

"Iie iie no iie no cold."

"Yes, cold, little one."

Shivering, she begged, "No, no more, I will stop, no more ice, please."

"You're lucky I ran out," he said flicking his hand at the shower. "Now missy, are you going to let me start the shower or are you not hungry?"

Emiko's stomach growled again like it had earlier, dissolving them both into laughter.

"I will be good."

"Good, 'cause I'm hungry, too." Xavier turned the water on and checked the temperature before setting Emiko under the spray and stepping in behind her. "Do you have clothes for dinner?"

"Hm, where are we going?"

"There's a nice diner not far from here, they do some of everything. It's not fancy but it's good."

"I have clothes then."

CHAPTER TWENTY-FOUR

An hour later found Xavier and Emiko in a 40's-style diner, sitting in the back booth. Xavier sat with his back to the wall, watching everyone who came in.

Emiko watched him over the top of the menu, which offered everything from a burger and fries to sushi, from spaghetti to tacos.

"I told you they had it all. Do you know what you want?"

"So many choices, I think I would like a steak taco salad."

"What do you want to drink?" Xavier asked trying to keep his calm.

Emiko watched her koishii struggle; she could see him flinch a little at each clatter and jump every time the door opened. Wanting to help, she set her menu down, took his hand in hers, and hummed the little song while stroking the back of his hand. Slowly, after she'd sung the song through a few times, Xavier was much calmer and stopped jumping as much.

"Is that the only one you know?" Xavier asked idly.

"Hmm, yes we do not have many songs like that in Japan. Americans seem to have very many."

"Yeah, there are a bunch, but I think a lot are from other places, just translated into English. We are a place for everyone to come to."

"A melting pot, yes? That is what it is called?" Emiko asked just to keep any conversation going.

"Yeah, sometimes I'm glad for it. Then other days I wish it was different, but there is nothing I can do either way." Xavier's look was becoming lost again but the waitress came over and he managed to shake it off.

"What you folks want tonight?" the girl drawled out in a thick Texas accent.

"She would like a taco salad with steak and I want the spaghetti with meatballs, please."

"Drinks?"

"Iced tea, no lemon and…" Xavier looked at Emiko but she was confused. "What do you want to drink, Emiko?"

"Um, just water please."

"'K, be a few."

"You okay?" Xavier asked, not sure why Emiko had gotten confused.

"Her accent was very hard to understand."

He laughed lightly, "Yes it was, but so is yours."

"If you say so."

"I do."

Emiko did not let go of his hand until dinner came, then she found his leg under the table and made sure her leg was touching his until it was time to leave.

"Do you want to call your roommates or go over and see if your father's been here?" Xavier asked. The day had been nice but they needed to remember why she had been there to start with.

"I think maybe we should go. I have to work tomorrow, and I will need to get something to wear."

"Alright, can you get us there from here?" Spending most of his time in his apartment meant he had little knowledge of how to get around town. The majority of his ventures out had been either to the liquor store five blocks from his house, the grocery store eight blocks away, or the base outside of town.

"Yes I can."

"Alright, lead on McDuff."

Emiko giggled again while she told Xavier how to get back to her apartment. She was trying not to think about what might be waiting for her there. Her father was not a patient man, but if he had to wait for something he wanted, he would.

Emiko froze when Xavier pulled in front of her building. Off to the side was a long black car, not a limo but definitely a car that came with its own driver. "Xavier, I, I am scared."

Xavier had seen the car as well. "I know, little one, just remember you are here on your own, but you are not alone. We could call Yvette and the other girls if you want or we could call Sam. He would come and tell your father not to bother you. It's up to you, but we will all be here for you."

Emiko sat in the Jeep for a long time trying to decide what would be best. She knew Xavier thought she was a strong person, but she was shaking so hard inside.

She was afraid if her father told her to pack and come, she would.

Finally, she decided that she would not, that she would tell her father that she was staying in America with her new family, a family who wanted her and who did not find her shameful, one who honored her by letting her be part of them.

"I will go up and talk to Otosan and be back in a little while. Will you be all right to wait here?" She asked, worried that Xavier would get upset sitting in his Jeep.

"I am a big boy, little one. I'll be fine. Are you sure you don't want me to come up with you?"

"Yes, I want you to come with me, but this is something I think I have to do by myself. I have to tell Father that I am staying here with my family." She turned and looked at Xavier for the first time since seeing the black car. Her eyes shone with unshed tears and her hands trembled a little.

"Emiko, it doesn't have to be them or us. Don't you think he can be reasoned with, that you can have all of us? Why do you have to lose your family?"

"I lost them two years ago when Kim left," she said quietly.

"Kim? Who's Kim?"

"Kim was…"

"Your betrothed, right?" he said, remembering what she had said in the restaurant.

"Yes," she confirmed.

"So he left you, he's the bastard. Why would you lose your family because of that?"

CHAPTER TWENTY-FIVE

Emiko took a deep breath and hoped Xavier would understand. "Kim was to take over the company someday. My father knew my brothers would be there but that they were not capable of running it. It was a heavy shame for my father. Kim was very smart and charismatic. My father knew right away that he would be able to do anything he wanted in life. He courted Kim in a way, getting him to work for the company and then he offered me to lift some of the shame of having sons that were not good enough. I would be good enough to get him a son that would carry on the Nara tradition, and then his grandsons would take over the company some day. Kim was ready, my father had made him a vice president, and we were to be married in two weeks. Kim left all of us and went to a competitor, taking with him all of the contacts he had made while with my father and some of my father's contacts. He was never going to stay or marry me, so my family thought the shame was mine for not making him happy enough to stay, for not being a good enough future wife for him."

"So your father is a rat bastard. This is not making it easier for me to stay here and let you go up there by yourself."

"It was not just my father; it was all of my family..."

"What did you want to be when you grew up?" Xavier asked, remembering that her life had been planned for her.

"A good wife," Emiko answered too quickly.

Exasperated, Xavier asked again, "What did you want to be when you grew up?"

"A gymnast. I loved watching the Olympics and the floor routines, but it was never to be."

"Why? Ok wait, don't answer that now. We'll talk about that later. Last time - you sure you don't want me..."

"No, I am sure; I need to see Otosan on my own. I need for him to see that I do not need them."

"Alright." Xavier pulled Emiko into a hug, rubbed her arms and kissed her cheek. "You are strong, and I am here if you want me."

"I know, thank you. I will be back soon."

Before she slipped out of his Jeep, Emiko leaned back over and gave Xavier an Eskimo kiss. He seemed dazed for a second, but then the laughter started. Emiko made it all the way to her door with the echo of his laughter in her ears; it was the most beautiful sound she had ever heard. Now she stood in front of her door preparing to do battle for the first time in her life, but the laughter was there to help her. She knew she needed to find a way to hear it every day. If she could, maybe Xavier would find himself again, stay with her, and not follow his friends.

Taking a deep breath, Emiko reached for the knob, paused for a moment, and then pushed the door open. She took one step into the living room and cried out, "Obāsan!" Sitting on her couch was her grandmother; off to the side of the room was her driver and companion, Yukio.

"Obāsan, what are you doing here? I thought the doctors said you should not travel."

"What do they know Emi-chan? They know nothing. Besides, they said I should not, not that I could not."

"Oh grandmother, it is so good to see you." Emiko sat down next to the frail woman. Her grandmother was the one person who had always been on her side. "Obāsan, why are you here? Otosan did not send you."

"No, that dithering fool knows nothing. How are you my dear, the mugging? You are alright?" Amarante Tanaka asked, leaning back a bit from her favorite grandchild. She may be a grandmother with health that was starting to fail her, but she could still see her akachan.

"I am fine, Obāsan. I was not hurt."

"I see that akachan. You must tell me what happened. Your father did not tell me anything, just that someone had tried to rob you and that they were arrested. The ass had no details."

"Grandmother, I did not give them any. I did not want them to worry and to come here."

"Emiko, they are stupid people. My daughter married badly. That Kim was never worthy of you. Emiko, look at me."

Emiko's head had dropped into a deep bow so that her grandmother could not see the shame she felt for letting her family down. "Emi-chan, look at Obāsan." The older woman did not continue until Emiko complied, looking at her grandmother from under her eyelashes.

"The shame was never yours and will never be yours. The shame is purely your father's. Yes, your brothers are not the, how do the Americans say it, the brightest bulb in the package, but they are still good boys. You are very smart and could have easily run the company, but your father never saw that, nor will he ever see it. Your father lives too far into the past. He has not learned that this is the twenty-first century and that you are as important as his precious Kim was, more so because you are his. Were his - I see that you will not be coming home," Amarante said speaking of Japan.

"I do, I, Obāsan, I do not understand."

"No, you would not my dear. You cannot see the glow you have around you. You see it, too, do you not, Yukio?"

"Hai kifujin," said Yukio.

"Who is your this friend that makes you glow with happiness?"

Her grandmother's question stunned her for a moment. Glow. Emiko struggled with the word and was glad Xavier was not there to hear it. She was afraid that he would fixate on the word as well. Glowing was something pregnant woman did, but she couldn't glow after a few hours could she?

"Emiko," her grandmother said, trying to get her attention, "are you alright?"

"Hai Obāsan. It has been a long few days. I...his name is Xavier St. Cloud. He was the one to rescue me from the mugger that day. Oh, Obāsan, he is such a brave man." Thinking of what she did know of Xavier's capture and all of the scars, a tear rolled down her cheek. "Oh Obāsan." Emiko suddenly crumpled into her grandmother's arms and cried.

Startled and concerned, Amarante held her sobbing granddaughter. Her companion disappeared into the kitchen returning with a glass of water and a dishcloth. "Emiko, what is wrong?" That only made her akachan cry harder. Deciding that the girl needed to get it out, she let her finish.

A few minutes later Emiko quieted. "Gomen nani, Obāsan."

"You have nothing to be sorry about. Though," she started, handing Emiko the glass and wiping away the tears, "you do have some explaining to do."

"Xavier is so strong, but the world has been so awful to him. He is in the American's Marine Corps. He is, oh, uh...um..." Emiko stumbled over the words, trying to remember what she had heard Sam tell Melissa. "He is in special ops," she finished, finally remembering. "He..."

"Your Xavier-san went on secret missions for the American government," Yukio furnished.

Emiko nodded. "He was captured on his last mission; he and his best friends were tortured for a long time. I am not sure how long; it hurts him to talk about it. His friends died but something intervened and he was saved. Almost."

"Almost?" grandmother asked.

"He says he died that day, that only his body survived. Obāsan, he has so many scars, and I think only a small portion is on his skin. I, we, I, I," Emiko paused, taking a deep breath. "I have seen all of them and the scars he sees with his eyes closed are far worse than the ones he sees when his eyes are open."

"Oh my akachan, my little one, you love him already."

Emiko's head popped up and then dropped back down. "Yes," she whispered.

"Emiko, this is a wonderful thing. I am so happy for you."

"You are?"

"Yes my child, my akachan. I am very happy for you. I want these things for you."

Yukio took the glass from Emiko and returned with it refilled. "Your grandmother wishes for your happiness every day, Emiko-san. You are her joy."

Emiko blushed at Yukio's observation, but his next statement made it grow even deeper. "And you are my joy. You give your grandmother light and that makes me happy. I have loved your grandmother for many years and I will love her for many more, God willing."

"Yukio, this is not the time to tell her about our relationship. It…"

"I don't know, I think it's as good a time as any," came a voice from the doorway.

CHAPTER TWENTY-SIX

"Xavier," Emiko jumped from the couch and ran to him as if they had been separated for months instead of forty-five minutes. "I am so sorry, I should not have left you for so long."

"Emiko, I am a big boy," he said aloud, then whispered into her ear, "I didn't jump at every shadow as much, little one. So I am going to hazard a guess and say it wasn't your dad's car." He stood looking between Amarante and Yukio.

"No, this is my grandmother, Amarante Tanaka and Yukio Mie, her..." Emiko stopped and shrugged her shoulders and finished, "her boyfriend."

Yukio beamed at the title. The man was in his 60's and had been in love with Amarante for over 30 years. He had seen her through her children leaving home, grandchildren being born and through the loss of her husband, a man who, until his death, had defined a cold husband.

"I am glad to meet you, Mr. St. Cloud." Amarante firmly gripped Xavier's outstretched hand, surprising him with her strength. "Emiko was telling us about you."

"Hm... was she?" Xavier was afraid of what Emiko might have said, and he wondered if he needed to watch out for her new grandpa. He was maybe ten years younger than the old lady was, but he sure as hell looked fit.

"Yes, she said you serve in your country's Marines, very honorable," said Yukio. "Moreover, she said that you were the one to save her from the robber. We are forever in your debt for saving koishii's granddaughter."

"Well, there's a word I know," Xavier said, chuckling and looking at Emiko.

The older couple was confused as Xavier laughed and Emiko blushed. "Did we miss a joke?" Amarante asked first.

"Emiko calls me koishii-chan, said my name didn't work very well for the nickname thing you guys do."

"Koto toiuada mei , Emiko-chan kare ga nani nitsuite hanashi teimasu?" (Nickname thing, Emiko-chan what is he talking about?)

"Yukio, we should use English," Emiko quickly said. "It would not be polite to speak when Xavier cannot understand us." Emiko also wanted to avoid any unpleasant memories for Xavier.

"Emiko, little one, it's okay I'm fine, don't worry about it. I can't avoid it for the rest of my life," Xavier said, his voice a little more strained than he would have liked, given that he was trying to put her at ease. He hoped that she would miss it and they could get her stuff and go. Being watched by the old man was starting to fray Xavier's nerves.

"It is not right, koishii-chan, and I will do what I am able, to help."

"Emiko, I have to get past it and I won't if I keep hiding or if you try to shield me from everything that might…"

"Might make you see those horrible things again. Koishii, it hurts me to see you with that look on your face. I know I will see it again, but if I can make it one less time then I will."

Overcome by her display of concern for him Xavier turned and said, "I'll be in the Jeep when you're ready to go." He took a step and stopped. "Or do you want to stay here, since I'm guessing your dad's not coming."

The thought stopped Emiko, too. "I, I do not know," she whispered, torn between wanting to be with Xavier and wanting to spend time with her grandmother.

"Fine, you know where I live."

The sound of the door slamming hard behind Xavier echoed though the small apartment.

CHAPTER TWENTY-SEVEN

"Oh," Emiko crumpled back on to the couch "what have I done?" Tears streaming down her face again.

"Emiko-san, what happened?" Yukio said, confused more now than before the man had come in.

Emiko wanted to tell them about Xavier, but she was afraid that they would not understand and tell her she should forget him. Pulling herself into a ball and hugging a pillow, she cried, "I have messed it up. Oh I, watashi hasorewo kotei surutameni naniwo suruka shiri masen. (I do not know what to do to fix it) He has flashbacks from when he and his friends were captured. He sees them die over and over again in front of his eyes. I have seen him relive it twice since I met him. Yesterday it was right here because I said yoroshii; his friends that died spoke many languages and Japanese was one. He knows a few words, and it triggered a flashback.

His friend, Sam, came, and Yvette and Sam kept him from hurting himself while Max was on his way here. When he was back, everyone was trying to decide where everyone should go. I did not want to leave Xavier alone with his nightmare, so I said I would go to his home. We, we..." blushing heavily again, she floundered.

Her grandmother thought she knew what was embarrassing the girl "Yukio-san, would you go and get us a snack and let us girls talk a bit?"

Yukio grinned at his love, getting the picture as well. "Yes koishii-chan, I like that, I may steal that one Emiko-san." He winked at Amarante and left.

"Now that it is just us girls you can tell me what has made you so..." Amarante stopped, leaving the question unfinished.

"We slept together last night but not how everyone thinks. He was very tired from his flashback. I was still very upset from the argument with Mama and thinking that Papa was going to come here and take me home. We both fell asleep very fast. We might have done more, but his alarm on his Jeep went off while we were kissing." Emiko blushed again and her grandmother blushed.

"Oh akachan, it is good to see you smile and blush like this. I know how it is between a man and woman; you have nothing to blush over." Amarante leaned over and kissed her forehead.

"I was so scared there was something wrong with me, my stomach hurt so badly, it kept twisting around on itself." Grandmother just smiled and listened. "I wanted him to kiss me, but when he moved to kiss me I moved back until the couch stopped me. Then he did and it was so very nice. Then the alarm," Emiko sighed "and when he got back from turning it off I had fallen asleep. He took me to his bed and I heard him tell Sam I was shivering so he got in bed to help me warm up. Today he was to go with his friend Sam to Max's for a barbeque. Max is a friend of Sam's and he is a psychologist. Things have been going fast for Xavier this week, I guess." She paused for a few minutes trying to remember all the things that had happened since she met Xavier. "He stopped a robbery on his first day out of his apartment in nearly three years. He found Sam, he went to see his old commander, he got a psychologist who has clearance to hear what he needs to say, he had a very bad flashback, we kissed, we went to the barbeque, we went home and we ..." Emiko's rambling stopped when she reached the part of her little time line that included their having sex.

"You made love like rabbits, I hope."

"Obāsan!" the girl said, embarrassed.

"What, you are a young girl who I would hope has a healthy appetite for sex."

"Grandmother."

"Oh, do not give me that, you are 25, you should have sex like bunnies."

Emiko dissolved into giggles as a quick flash of Xavier being a soft bunny popped into her mind.

"So you two got it on, as the Americans say, yes?"

Emiko giggled again and nodded her head, "Yes."

"Was he good?" That question was followed by another round of giggles.

CHAPTER TWENTY-EIGHT

"I hope he does not hear you two giggle after that question," Yukio said, returning with bento boxes.

"Oh you found..."

"Yes, I found it right where you told your grandmother it would be. I mentioned you and they were very quick to make us a snack. Did I give you girls enough time?"

Emiko blushed once more and Amarante nodded her head. "We got the important stuff said."

"Okay, well being the father-figure here, you were careful, yes?"

Emiko nodded and then stopped and shook her head no.

"Yes or no, cannot be both."

"The first time we..." blushing again, she could not say it, "but the second time" she started again, "we forgot."

"Emiko-san, are you alright?"

"I am fine, I have no worries about the, um..." she was getting tired of being confused and being so shy about everything. She took a deep breath, lifting her shoulders and letting them drop heavily as she built the courage to be less shy, "I am sure Xavier is healthy." She took one more breath and said, "And he had no reason to worry about me because..." Emiko wavered again as she played with the blanket from yesterday. Smelling Xavier's scent on it, she pushed on. "He was my first. He was worried that I may become pregnant."

"He is worried or scared?"

"I do not know, Yukio-san, he said something when he went into the store about maybe someday, but not now. I told him earlier that I would worry when there was something to worry about."

Amarante pulled her granddaughter into her arms and held her. "That may be one of the reasons he was angry when you said you were not sure if you wanted to go to his home, Emi-chan. He is scared also and for many reasons, it appears. You changed his world."

"He says I am his light, his sun, he says that he has been in the dark for so long he knows the difference. He says that I am strong and brave. Obāsan, I do not feel strong or brave." Emiko was crying again, "I feel so shy and scared of everything. I, I was, I wanted to come up here and tell Otosan that I was not going home with him and that I was staying here with my new family, but I was so afraid that as soon as he demanded it I would say yes and go with him, hurting Xavier."

"You are strong akachan, you have been strong everyday of your life. You just did not know that was what you were being because no one ever pointed it out to you before. You could have crawled to Kim asking him to take you back, as I know your father wanted you to do, but your father was smart enough to know that you would not do it. He knew sending you here was the best for you even if he would never say it."

"Okasan said I was going to America to live with…"

"I know, she told me that it was her idea, but my daughter has never had an original idea in her life," Amarante said with contempt. "Her father coddled her and gave her everything, so she thinks she deserves everything. Your mother only wanted your father because one of her schoolmates wanted him. Your mother was the prettier of the two, so she won. It was your father who sent you here; it was just your mother who told you to go."

"I am glad I am here. I have many friends here. I would like you to meet them." Emiko asking with trepidation," Are you staying long?"

"Yes akachan, we are staying for some time."

The sadness in her Obāsan's voice scared her. "Obāsan, are you well? You are not..."

"No little one, I am not dying yet."

"You are..."

"It is me, Emiko-san," Yukio spoke up. "I have colon cancer. There is a specialist here at the hospital that has had very high success with removing all the tumors. He has agreed to see me."

"Yukio-san, but you are so young yet."

"Oh Emiko-san, you are good for people, you are a ray of positive light."

"But Obāsan would be lost without you, Yukio-san, you have been with her for so many years."

"I know Emi-chan," he said using the family nickname. "I do not plan on leaving her when we are finally free to show ourselves. Now, enough about my problem, what do we do about your man?"

"I am afraid I have ruined..."

"No, now none of that nonsense, Emi-chan. We will take you to your koishii-chan and you will show him that he is important to you. Come, little one."

"I have to get some clothes for work first. That was why we came, but when we saw your car..."

"You thought it was his."

"Hai."

"That is alright, now you know it was us."

"Maybe we could keep your man company tomorrow while you are at work, Emiko-san." Yukio fell back into the habit of using the more formal name.

"I will ask. He has a hard time around people, especially people he does not know."

"You ask, Emi-chan," her grandmother said. "He is free to say no but there can be no yes if the question is not asked."

"Yes, Obāsan."

CHAPTER TWENTY-NINE

An hour later Emiko stood at Xavier's door, bag on the floor, Obāsan and Yukio-san's phone number programmed in her cell phone and her hand raised to knock. There had been no lights on in any of the windows; she was afraid that he was asleep. She did not want to knock and scare him.

She was so afraid of hurting him again by doing something without thinking. Praying that it would be all right, Emiko knocked. There was a thud and the sound of shuffling on the other side of the door. When the door opened, Xavier stood there, bottle in hand, tears streaming down his face.

"What do you want?" he snarled.

"Koishii-chan." Emiko went into full mother mode, taking the bottle and wiping away the Marine's tears. "What are you doing sitting in the dark, drinking?" She did not ask about the crying, sure he did not know he was.

Slurring his words Xavier answered, "You left me. What was I supposed to do?

My light was gone." He dropped into the chair and looked away from Emiko.

"I am not gone and I did not leave you. I have not seen my grandmother in two years. I wanted to go with you, but I wanted to stay and talk with Obāsan. I have missed her so much. I did not know they were going to stay. They would like to see you tomorrow, if you are willing. They understand that you do not like to be around people a lot. Obāsan is very happy that I found you."

"Why do they want to spend time with me?" Xavier asked, still not looking at Emiko.

"Because they see that I love you. They want to know the one who makes me glow." Emiko was tired of Xavier turning away from her each time she tried to see his face; she clasped it between her hands and turned it to her. She knew if he did not want her to move him, she could not. "I love you, so they love you."

Shuddering at Emiko's statement, Xavier said, "Emiko, I am so messed up."

"Shush," she said sitting down on his lap. "Shush." She kissed his forehead and when he started to talk once more, she kissed him again. "You are wounded, yes," she said, kissing him again, "but you have not had the right medicine to heal. I hope now you do."

Xavier couldn't believe Emiko was back in his apartment. He was sure she would be on the next plane with her grandmother. However, she was sitting here on his lap kissing him, telling him she loved him and that her grandmother and her friend were staying and wanted to see him tomorrow. He was so happy his light was back. He was sure he couldn't go another day without her. He had been so desperate when she didn't come with him tonight, he went looking for his gun, determined to finish what had started three years ago, but when he picked it up it felt light - too light. Popping the clip out and finding it empty of its seventeen rounds, he went to the closet looking for his spare ammo. Instead of the box, he found a band-aid box. Baffled Xavier grabbed a bottle of Jim and sat in the dark. An hour later, he heard a knock on the door. Too drunk to care, he opened the door after tripping over the coffee table and the edge of the couch. And his world was bright again. He wanted to drop to his knees and hug her. Instead something made him try to hurt her with his words, but she didn't take the bait. She was strong again, and now, now she was kissing him quiet.

"Emiko I, I need to tell you something," he said putting his head on her shoulder so she couldn't kiss him again. He was tempted to let her, but if they were going to start a relationship he had to tell her about the colonel's offer. He had to tell her that if he took it he might lose what little headway he had made. Hugging her as he had wanted to a minute ago, he told her, "I saw my commanding officer yesterday. I am still in the reserves, not active duty. I have been asked to go and interrogate a prisoner."

"A prisoner?" she asked confused again.

"Yes, they want me to go and question the leader of the group that..." he paused, swallowing hard, "they want me to question the man who killed Lance and Shawn."

"Why?" she whispered.

"Because the colonel thinks I deserve a shot at getting a little back from him. He thinks that I can break him where apparently others have failed. I do have 'the supposed to being dead' shock thing going."

"Will it save people?"

"Maybe, they think he has information about another attack. Not an imminent one, but one coming up soon."

"Where is he?" she asked.

"In Afghanistan."

"When will you leave?" she whispered, her voice steady, but she knew if she thought too much she would cry.

"I don't want to go."

"Your colonel is right; you need to go. You need to face the man again and make him tell you the things he knows so that you can save the people who might be hurt by his attack. If you did not and there was an attack next week, it would hurt you as much as losing your friends. If Max thinks you will be all right, then I think that you should go."

"I might not."

"You will come back, and I will be here when you return, koishii-chan."

"I'm…Emiko, I'm afraid that if I go I will lose what I have started to get back."

"You will be fine; I think you will come back stronger. I think you should do one thing though while you have this man, one thing for me."

Xavier leaned back as far as the chair would let him and cocked one eyebrow, "And that is?" he asked when she didn't go on.

"I think you should walk up and give him one of your Eskimo kisses and tell him that he is a bad shot."

The stunned look on Xavier's face was too much for Emiko, she had to laugh.

"You want me to what?"

"I think you should kiss him like this," she said, leaning in and rubbing her nose on his, "and tell him he is a bad shot. Also I think you should tell him your girlfriend said so and that she says thank you for being a lousy shot." Tilting her head to the side, Emiko hoped she had gotten the right slang term.

"Lousy shot?" Xavier parroted back.

"Lousy is not right?" afraid she had gotten it wrong after all.

"No, lousy is right."

"Then yes, you should tell him that. Will that not throw him off his game?" she asked, again hoping she used the right term.

"How did you know he shot me?"

Emiko hugged Xavier's shoulders. "The day you had your flashback you talked a great deal. It sounded as if you were giving a report, you gave many details," she told him, hoping that her admission would help, not hinder.

"Oh," was all he had to say. "I guess I don't have to tell you about it then."

"When you are ready, I would like to hear what happened. Well, that is not what I meant. I would be..."

"I get it, little one, if I need to spout I can come to you."

"Yes, koishii-chan, I would like to know how you got your many scars," she said, "but when you are ready. I can wait."

"Emiko, let's go to bed."

"Yoroshii, I, uh..."

"It's fine, little one. I am fine, stop doing that."

"I do not want to hurt you."

Kissing her silent as he carried her to the bedroom, he set her on the bed.

Picking up the box of condoms and setting them on the pillow, he said, "No more taking chances right now. If I come back…"

"When you come back," she interrupted.

"When I come back," he said, "then we can talk about a lot of things, but for now…" He kissed her again and helped her undress.

"I know you do not want me to see them, but if we turned off the light, I would not be able to see them."

"What are you getting at, little one?" He could tell she wanted something but was too shy to ask.

"I want to undress you."

"If we turn off the lights there won't be anything for you to see."

"I know, it is just that I want to do it for you." She shrugged and sighed sounding silly to herself.

"Go ahead."

"What, I…"

"Go ahead. You have seen them and you will see them again. If I can't handle it, then we'll turn off the light."

Emiko scrambled off the bed and knelt at Xavier's feet, unlacing his boots as she had in the restaurant. She pulled them off quickly and his socks found their way to the floor. Still kneeling but rising up, she reached out and undid his belt and the button to his pants. Biting her lip, she unzipped the zipper. Her face wrinkled in thought when she reached to pull the camouflaged pants off, but Xavier lifted himself up and she pulled them down. She left his boxers for now. After throwing the pants over her shoulder, and smiling at the light laughter her actions had caused, she found the first one of his scars.

She had a plan. She was going to kiss every scar and give him a good memory to replace the bad with when he thought about them.

CHAPTER THIRTY

The first scar she found was on his right knee, a long and slightly jagged scar that looked as though it must have been painful when he got it. She leaned down kissing it from top to bottom. She felt Xavier shiver. She set that foot to the floor and picked up his left. There she found a wide rounded scar half way up his shin, kissing it from left to right.

Emiko stood after setting his left leg down. She reached out and took hold of the hem of his shirt, looking at him to make sure he was all right. He nodded to her once and she pulled the shirt over his head, throwing it so it landed in a ball on the chair at the far corner of the room. He laughed again and she smiled.

This time she pushed on him until he fell back onto the bed. She took his right arm in her hand and kissed up the scar that was on the inside of his forearm. She lay the arm back on the bed and straddled his chest to reach his right shoulder. She could feel Xavier's cock press into her butt cheek. She was happy this was keeping him aroused, but she had a lot of work to do before she would kiss the last scar. Again, Emiko kissed from left to right on the scar his right shoulder bared. It was a long scar, which took up the length of the broad shoulder. It was smoother than some of the ones on his other shoulder, but it still looked painful.

She debated for a second whether to go down his chest or across to his shoulder but decided on down. The thin scars were short, none really longer than an inch. She placed a single kiss on every one starting on the right side working down and left as she went. When she ran out there, she picked up his left arm and kissed two ragged scars, the worst of the ones she had kissed to that point. Leaning a little to the left, Emiko began at the top of his shoulder and kissed each heavy, thick scar. Up close, she could see where some of the suture marks were and she held her breath hoping she would not cry for the pain he had to have lived in while this healed. Once she finished with the scars she assumed were from the debris of the attack that had freed him, she kissed the gunshot scar. Being so close to his heart, she lingered there. She could hear the fast beat of it and, with a smile, she wiggled slowly across his groin and she heard it speed up a little more. Reaching up she kissed his lips.

"I don't have a scar there, little one."

"I know, I want you to roll over. I am not done yet, koishii-chan."

He shook his head, "No 'cause you will have to move and I don't want you to."

"I will be back, I am not going away."

"You're going away from him." Xavier pouted shaking his hips so that she moved across his cock again.

"Only for a moment, I will not be far." Emiko moved to kneel next to him on the bed.

"Hm," he said rolling on to his stomach, "should have started back there instead of making me lie on this thing."

"I am sorry. I do not think about the anatomy part of this idea. I only wanted to give you happy memories for your scars." Settling over his ass, Emiko leaned to his left shoulder and kissed the remainder of the scars from the debris and lingered over the mate to the gunshot wound.

One long thin scar brushed up along the gunshot scar and she followed it down to the maze of long thin scars on his back. She kissed all of them and found a circle pattern of little round scars. She kissed each one quickly as you would, playing with a small child. The response was what she was looking for; she was shaken as Xavier laughed out load.

"Little one, that surprisingly enough, tickles."

"Really? I will remember this for another time."

"Oh crap, I'm done for aren't I?"

"We will see." A long heavy scar ran down his back that looked like the thin ones, but was so much different at the same time; she carefully kissed it from top to bottom. That only left two scars she had not kissed, the mate on his arm and the one on his hip she had saved for last. Slipping down off his back Emiko lay down and kissed the one on his arm.

"Koishii-chan?"

"Yes, little one?"

"Roll back over."

Xavier sighed and did as she asked, for whatever reason her kissing all of his scars had made him harder than he had been in his entire life if he thought about it. His cock had not appreciated being laid upon.

"I have one left."

"No, little one, there are a few more but you can't see them."

Emiko thought he meant the ones in his heart so she leaned to kiss him on his heart. When she sat back up there was a smile but he shook his head no.

Confused again, Emiko looked Xavier up and down "I did not,"

Then he reached and moved a lock of hair aside so she could see there were little ones under the hair. "I've got about ten up there, hidden by my hair. I'm not shaving it so you can see them though, little one."

Emiko leaned forward and instead kissed him ten times on the lips. "I think that will cover them," he said trying to hold her down to him.

"No, I have one more," Emiko said wiggling free. Taking a breath of courage Emiko pulled his boxers off and showed the final scar. She switched sides of the bed, getting off and walking around, knowing that if she tried to climb over him he would stop her.

He must have figured out what she was doing because he laughed once more. When she sat down next to his hip, he laughed harder. Xavier tried to grab her hands so that he could pin her to the bed, but she was much more agile than he had given her credit for. She pulled away and lay on her side so that her face was even with his hip. "Will you please let me finish?" she asked.

He heard the plea in her voice and let her finish. "Ok, ok, I won't touch you 'till you're done." He gave in.

Rising up on her elbows, Emiko kissed the last scar on his right hip, so close to his manhood she carried on kissing up to the top of his cock.

He hissed again, when she touched him. And before she could keep up with what was going on, she was on her back and he was buried in her.

"God, Emiko, oh God."

Knowing a little more what to do this time she wrapped her legs around

Xavier's waist and met him thrust for thrust.

"Oh God, you're going to be the death of me, little one."

"Iie no, I will be the life of you." She reached up and pulled him down into a long kiss.

Hours later Emiko woke up to something poking her in the face. She batted it away only to have it slide back into her cheek. Picking it up to see what it was, she gasped when she realized it was the condom box that still only had one missing.

"Yeah, I know, it's been taunting me for the last ten minutes," Xavier said from his position half on and half off her chest.

"I do not think it will matter, koishii-chan. We are going to be with each other for many years, yes?"

"I hope so, but you should get a chance to do things."

"I can do things and be a mother too, if that is the way it is to be."

"Are you sure?"

"Yes."

"All right." Hugging his lover, Xavier took a staggered breath. "I will call the colonel in the morning."

"Good."

"And I will see if I can handle lunch or something with your, your..."

"Obāsan," she supplied.

"Yes, your Obāsan and your step."

"Oh, ojisan," she said supplying the word for grandfather.

"Your Obāsan and your ojisan.

"Yes, Amarante and Yukio," she said reminding him of their names.

"Question: if they did not come to take you home, why are they here?"

"Yukio has colon cancer, and there is a specialist here that they are sure can help."

"Oh, is he... does he... hm... what are his odds?"

"I do not know. They did not mention it, but they seemed in high spirits so I will hope for the best."

"Hmm. Throw the box in the closet, will you? It's driving me nuts," Xavier said drowsily.

Emiko picked up the offending box and hurled it into the closet and with a very nice thwack, it hit the wall.

"Thanks." Xavier's eyes were too heavy to open.

"Sleep my koishii-chan, sleep." Emiko started singing.

"Nen nen cororiyo, ocororiyo
boya wa yoiko da, nen ne shina
boya no omori wa, doko e itta
ano yama koete, sato e itta
sato no miyage ni nani morota
den den daikon ni, sho no fue."

CHAPTER THIRTY-ONE

Xavier was dreaming. He was sure he was dreaming; he better be dreaming.

"Yes, man, you're dreaming; well, you're not dead, we'll say that."

"Dream." Xavier shook his head, closed his eyes and opened them again. They were still there.

"Guys?!"

"Yes."

"What gives?"

Lance and Shawn looked at each other, they had always had a way of having a whole conversation with looks alone and it seemed here, wherever here was, they still did. When they looked back at him, he knew this was a dream, but they were real.

"We have tried to get you to listen for three years. You have to stop beating yourself up over this," Lance said waving his hand back and forth between him and Shawn.

"You need to live again. You are going to take the mission from the colonel, and you are going to come home and make Emiko a happy woman," Shawn said.

"I miss you guys so much," Xavier said, "I can't…"

"We know, we see it every day and every night. We try to keep you from remembering, but you're so damned determined that there's nothing we can do to stop you," Shawn told him.

"Until two nights ago," Lance chimed in.

Xavier shook his head confused.

"Emiko was there and she kept you from remembering; she kept you from having more nightmares."

"I think I love her."

"We know we do," Lance said with a big smile on his face. His hair was how it had looked before they joined the Corps, long enough to spike up and bleached almost white underneath with his natural dark blond/light brown coloring showing through. Lance was always dark skinned - he could carry a tan for months. Shawn's hair was colored the same as Lance's but much shorter, and he too was tanned. Both wore rings they had seen online from a shop on the west coast called Tsunami Beads. They looked like double sided, double ended crosses bent so the ends would meet, the stones were of shades similar to their partner's eyes. The pair had never worn them on base but when they were home, putting on the rings was the first thing they would do, even before they took off their shoes.

"I know you would like her, Lance, she is…"

Lance interrupted his friend, "Oh the Asian bit is just a bonus, and we love her because she has done exactly what you told her she has done. She has brought light back into your life."

"I almost lost that light earlier," he said mostly to himself thinking about the missing bullets.

"No you didn't," Shawn said emphatically.

"Huh?"

"Watched Sam." Shawn smiled.

Suddenly understanding, Xavier said, "The band aid box."

"Yep, Saver."

"Was too…" he started to say something but Lance interrupted once more.

"Too damn shit-faced again to get it."

"Hm, guess I was." Xavier remembered the nametag Sam had given him years ago in the shape of a band-aid that had read Saver.

"You need to go back to Emiko, Saver, and you need to let her make you happy again," Shawn said.

"Oh and we agree with her. We think you should fuck with his head," Lance threw out.

"What?" Xavier asked, not getting the sudden topic change.

Shawn shook his head, walked over to Xavier, took a hold of his head, and gave him an Eskimo kiss before Xavier could react.

"Oh! Oh! Why didn't you just say so? Why did you have to kiss me?" Xavier joked with his friend and wiped the kiss from his nose.

"Oh, I could kiss you, big boy," glancing down, Shawn laughed, "but I think he might get mad at me," he finished, looking at Lance.

Xavier looked down too and it dawned on him for the first time since the dream started that he was as naked as he was on the bed.

"Damn, least I could have done was given myself some clothes."

"We don't care, it's just good to see you," both men said from either side of Xavier.

"Guys."

"Oh quit," they said as they both wrapped their arms around their friend. Hugging him between them, their familiar warmth cocooned Xavier. "We have missed you but don't come see us too soon, okay?" Shawn told him.

"We can wait; man, we can wait a long time," Lance said.

"Now it's time to wake up and make a couple phone calls," Shawn whispered to his friend, and pushed him toward consciousness.

***

Once awake, Xavier looked at the nightstand. He sighed and opened the drawer. There were only three things in the drawer, a ring with light green stones, a ring with light blue stones, and a set of dog tags. He took all three out and set the dog tags on his stomach.

Looking at the rings, a single tear rolled down his cheek. He didn't even try to stop it. Emiko did though, kissing it away.

"Xavier?"

"These were their rings. We shared an apartment before," Xavier's voice cracked but he kept going. "As soon as we got back, they would put their rings on, before they even took off their coats or shoes. They loved each other so much. The world shouldn't be without that love Emiko."

"We will just make sure that everyone knows that it still exists and share our love with everyone."

"I'll try to share it but I was never good at sharing my toys as a kid." He smiled and kissed Emiko's shoulder, the only part he could reach without moving.

Emiko did move though and took the rings from Xavier and set them on the nightstand, she picked up Xavier's dog tags, looked at them, then pulled them on. She pulled her hair out from underneath the beaded chain and looked at Xavier. She smiled and leaned down and kissed him...she never made it to work that day, but then Yvette hadn't expected her to anyway.

CHAPTER THIRTY-TWO

THREE DAYS LATER

"Well, well, who do we have here?" Xavier said walking into the cell holding his former torturer. He watched as all of the color drained out of the man's face. With a smile, he walked up to the man chained to the table and chair, and leaned forward. The man, use to in-the-face tactics, stood his ground and didn't move away. This suited Xavier just fine as he said, "My fiancée says I should thank you for being a lousy shot, and she said I should do this," Xavier leaned farther in and rubbed his nose twice across the man's nose, "and my friends you killed agree."

The man jerked back as if he had been slapped, trying to reach his face with his hands, but the restraints wouldn't allow it.

"So now about those plans you guys have for…"

***

13 DAYS LATER

"Obāsan, where is he? His plane landed hours ago." Emiko asked absolutely rubbing Xavier's dog tag around her neck.

Stilling her granddaughter's hand, "Emi-chan, they have protocols they must adhere to."

"I, I am so nervous."

"Koishii, it will be fine; he will be here soon."

Emiko and her grandmother were waiting on the base in the colonel's office. They had been there for almost two hours waiting for Xavier's plane to land and now that it had, it was almost unbearable for Emiko. Almost two weeks without Xavier was making it hard for her to think.

So lost in her misery she did not see him walk past the window of the office, but when the door opened and he was there, she jumped from the couch and all but threw herself into his arms.

"Koishii-chan, koishii-chan! I, I, oh, I have missed you so."

"Down, little one, I'm right here."

Tears streamed down Emiko's face, "I have missed you."

"I know, little one, I have missed you, too."

Leaning back and looking at Xavier, Emiko could see her love had not slept well. He looked as bad as he did the first time they had met: pale with dark shadows under his eyes. This time though there was a light in his eyes and his body was not slumped in defeat.

"I, we would like to take you to dinner if you think you are up to it?" Emiko asked stepping back to show her grandmother was there.

"Where's Yukio?" Xavier hoped the man's health had not worsened.

"He's resting. He starts his first round of chemo tomorrow; they want to try to shrink the tumor some before they try to take it out."

"Oh, but he's good, Amarante?"

"Yes, he is good."

"Let's go to dinner then."

***

Later that night when the two were wrapped around one another again, Emiko wondered how to ask what was on her mind. Xavier was absent-mindedly rubbing his hand over her belly, they would not know for a few more weeks if she was pregnant but Xavier thought he could use some pregnant belly rub practice either way.

"Koishii-chan?" she began tentatively.

"Yes little one?" Xavier had heard the tone in her voice and wondered about it.

"You called your mother before you left, yes?"

"Yes," he said drawing out the word.

"And you called her when you got here?"

"Stateside," he offered the word he thought she was looking for.

"Yes, you called her stateside."

"Yes, why?"

"She called a few days ago and I answered."

"That's fine." Xavier sighed.

"She asked if we were coming to the wedding."

"That's not fine."

Emiko had been going over in her head all the things she could say to him, but they all escaped her now.

"Koishii-chan, weddings are not dark."

"I know, but I still am..."

"Only a little," she offered softly "and if I go with you, you will have your portable sun with you."

Xavier laughed lightly. "Yes I will. Are you trying to ask if I will introduce you to my family?"

"Ummm, yes?" she said with a smile.

"Fine, I will make arrangements tomorrow to fly us home for the wedding."

"Yes, thank you, thank you, thank you. I like your mother; she is a very nice woman."

"She's just happy I met someone."

"Hm, maybe, but she is still the nicest mother I have ever met."

"Having heard some of the stories from Amarante I understand that."

"Koishii-chan, how far away is the wedding?"

"About three weeks, I think."

"Hmm, we should know by then." Emiko placed her hand over his on her stomach.

"Yeah, we should know if we are going to make her an Obāsan."

"I think she would like that."

"Well, then maybe we should try again, just in case it didn't take last time."

"Yes, we should practice a lot; they say practice makes perfect." Emiko nodded to herself.

"Yes, they do," Saver said, kissing his savior to distraction once more.

ABOUT THE AUTHOR

Yasmina is from a small town in the middle of...naw you know better. Yasmina is originally from Vancouver, WA and then by way of the Navy and college ended up in Grays Harbor County with her husband and her two kids and now the two black cats. Yes, she has two of the furry beasts.

During the day, she keeps the people happy or tries to anyway. At night, she tries to keep her sanity by escaping aforementioned family to write down what the evil muses have shoved in her brain all day.

She waits for the graduation of her kids (one imminent and one not so imminent) so that the house will become quite.

She listens to an eclectic mix of music when she writes, anything from Shinedown to Nora Jones and a little of The Asteroids Galaxy Tour thrown in for the fun of it.

Her sarcastic sense of humor has and will continue to get her in trouble but hey who cares?

Yasmina has been writing between cries of MOM and YASMINA for ten years and plans to write for many more. Her first published stories were fanfiction for her favorite TV series but the first story she tried her hand at was Cassandra's Heart now available on Amazon.com, BarnesandNoble.com, Smashwords.com and soon in print.

Follow Yasmina Kohl on Twitter, Facebook, Shelfari, Linkedin, Librarything, and Goodreads. The user name for all the sites is yasminakohl.

Or drop her an email and let her know what you think at yasminakohl@gmail.com.

Made in the USA
San Bernardino, CA
14 March 2014